SHIRA & ESTHER'S
DOUBLE DREAM
DEBUT

SHIRA & ESTHER'S
DOUBLE DREAM
DEBUT

Anna E Jordan

BY **ANNA E. JORDAN**

Dream Big!

chronicle books
san francisco

FOR
ISAAC & ETHAN
AND
MOM & DAD

Library of Congress Cataloging-in-Publication Data available.

ISBN 978-1-7972-1565-5

Manufactured in China.

Design by Kathryn Li and Jay Marvel.
Typeset in Adobe Caslon Pro.

10 9 8 7 6 5 4 3 2 1

Chronicle Books LLC
680 Second Street
San Francisco, California 94107

Chronicle Books—we see things differently.
Become part of our community at www.chroniclekids.com.

HAVE I GOT A STORY FOR YOU.

OVERTURE

HOUSE ON A HILL

DID YOU EVER NOTICE that when people build a town, they put the most important things on a hill? It's true. Where are your universities? Where do the bosses live? Where are the fancy gardens? On a hill. Am I right? Of course I'm right. So it is in the town of Idylldale.

Now, if there's one thing I know, it's sandwiches, and if I were to make an Idylldale sandwich, I'd start with two thick slices of humor spread with a thin layer of history. Next, alternate a quarter-pound desire with some faith. Grind a generous amount of wonder on top and add a pinch of woe . . . delicious!

So where is Idylldale? How do you get there? Ah, my children, *mayne kinder*, hear that *clang*? That's the Idylldale trolley now. Drop this token in the collector, and take a seat. We'll take a tour. First stop, the theater—the Heights.

"The Heights" is actually the lowest place in town. That's ironic, isn't it? Look, just beyond it, there are the railroad tracks, and beyond them, the laborers and their families who live and work in the shadow of the textile mill.

But here at the Heights the awning lights are a beacon. *Come to me*, the lights say. *Bask in my warmth. For inside, there will be music, bright costumes, and laughter. We speak your language; we are your heritage.* And the people of Idylldale come.

The smell of hot buttered popcorn wafts over the puppet matinee ticket line. Children in short pants and caps or dresses and bows wait with their parents to laugh together at the matinee. At night, a grown-up audience fills the Heights when the Yiddish theater troupe performs. What's Yiddish? Imagine that you combined the languages of Eastern Europe and Germany in a pot with Hebrew and let it simmer. That warm chicken soup of a language would be Yiddish.

For years, the people of Idylldale watched Yiddish stories and sang Yiddish songs they heard at the Heights. On Saturday nights, after an otherwise drab week, the workers and bosses would rub shoulders at the Heights. They all wore what the actors in the troupe deemed fashionable. They even collected and traded cards with the actors' pictures. And if the actors made it big in New York City? *Oy gevalt*, in Idylldale, it was as if the actors were royalty!

But now, people from both sides of the railroad tracks come to the theater less and watch their televisions more. Many of the children no longer understand Yiddish. Audiences who used to go to the Heights now see their shows at Scheinfeld's. What is Scheinfeld's? Hold your horses, we're on our way.

The town hall, hospital, and Trolley Transfer Station anchor the center of Idylldale where, on street corners, men with aprons rearrange their fruits and vegetables.

On side streets, homes are shoved together like third-class travelers. Fire escapes crisscross the fronts of brick apartment buildings, and carved brownstone leaves accent the roofs and doors of skinny row houses.

Hang on to the hand straps, now, this bridge over the Idylldale River is bumpy. Up, up, up the hill we go!

Here, the houses have more room to breathe. The trees spread their limbs, and the pavement gives way to an emerald carpet. Look! It's Scheinfeld's Resort and Cottages—a sprawling vacation oasis with bellboys and housekeepers scurrying back and forth to fill the needs of each well-to-do guest.

You see the shuffleboard area? The tennis courts? The spa? Grown-ups at the gazebo learn fancy dances with names like waltz, foxtrot, and tango. At oak-shaded picnic tables, children knot string bracelets and paint macaroni necklaces. The *tummler*, the funmaker, starts a cannonball contest to make the guests laugh and get them swimming. There's a bellboy carrying luggage for a celebrity from television who will perform in the big Thursday night show.

Scheinfeld's is on the hill. But it's not at the tippy-top of the hill. Why?

Because for some folks here, there is still higher to go. On Friday night and Saturday morning, the guests at Scheinfeld's who want to be closest to God walk along a tree-lined path, up a wide wooden staircase to Idylldale's most important house—the synagogue, where Stars of David decorate circular windows in its dome.

Right now, no one is at the synagogue on the hill because its religious leader, Rabbi Epstein, is at the hospital. He paces back and forth in the waiting room with Mrs. Epstein's brother. Why are they pacing? They are waiting for Rabbi Epstein to become a father and for Mrs. Epstein's brother to become an uncle. That's right, Mrs. Epstein is having a baby!

And here she is! The baby is rosy cheeked with a small tuft of dark hair on her *keppie*. *Keppie* rhymes with *peppy* and is Yiddish mixed with English for "head." Isn't that a cute word? As cute as a baby's *keppie*. She is *so* beautiful that the nurse has Papa, Mama, and Uncle Coop all crowd around the bed to take a picture. *Pop!* goes the flash. Boy, oh boy, has that baby got lungs! Listen to her wail.

And she's not the only one wailing! Right down the hall from Mrs. Epstein's hospital room is Fanny Rosenbaum's room. No one calls her Miss Rosenbaum, though. They call her by her stage name: Red Hot Fanny.

There's no Mr. Red Hot Fanny. There *was* a man. A nice traveling salesman, Mel, who fell in love with Fanny as soon as he saw her on the stage at the Heights. Fanny loved him too—body and soul. But when fame came calling in the form of a national television tour, she told him it was over. Fanny's one true love was the stage. And Mel? He was gone, heartbroken, before she could tell him about this new bundle of joy.

Fanny has always said, "For a little love, you pay all your life," and she's paying now. Fanny wails and pushes and pushes and wails and out comes a second baby this night in Idylldale.

The rabbi and Mrs. Epstein name the first baby, the one with strong lungs and dark hair on her *keppie*, Shira, which means "song." Rabbi Epstein hopes that Shira will sing next to him on the *bima* in his synagogue on the hill. Shira drinks her mother's milk this night as if there's no tomorrow—and there won't be. Oh, don't worry. Shira will be fine, but Mrs. Epstein will die by sunrise.

Red Hot Fanny, on the other hand, will be strong as an ox tomorrow, as will her baby. Did I mention that her baby had dark hair on her *keppie* too? I didn't? Well sue me; I'm telling you now. Fanny's baby had dark hair the same as Shira and a star-shaped mole on her neck that was all her own. But while Shira wails, Fanny's baby lets out the gentlest cry. Fanny is sure that the baby will be a star and perform beside her on the stage at the Heights. And so Fanny names her child Esther, a star of the Jewish people.

Oy vey. Are those parents wrong.

ACT I

CHAPTER ONE

THE HEIGHTS

ON SATURDAY NIGHT, THE Sabbath, or the Jewish day of rest, is over. When does night begin? Some people in Idylldale say it's when three stars shine in the sky. These families separate the day of rest, Shabbat in Hebrew or Shabbos in Yiddish, from the workweek by lighting braided candles, smelling sweet spices, drinking wine, and saying prayers.

For others in Idylldale, night is as soon as the bright lights of the Heights flicker and blaze.

To ride the trolley, you need a token; to get into the Heights, you need a ticket. And who takes your ticket? Levi, the *shtarker*, or strong man, stands at the polished brass doors each Saturday evening to make sure that everyone has a ticket and that everyone in the audience conducts themselves in a respectable manner. Now, Levi doesn't ask for a ticket or even look up from his newspaper as Benny Bell runs past, because Benny is theater family.

A newspaper flaps in Benny's hand as he runs through the brass doors, down the tattered red carpet, and leaps to the stage—a feat his fourteen-year-old body can now manage. He halts for a moment, as he always does, to wish on the ceiling mural of clouds the color of salmon. He hopes that someday he might be featured on a stage like this one, with its ornate carved and gilded proscenium. He pushes past the red velvet curtains calling, "Esther?" but no one is backstage. Passing ladders and lights and jogging down the stairs to the dressing rooms, he calls again, "Esther? Don't let Fanny see the evening paper." After all the yelling, his staccato knock is irrelevant. The door opens enough for Benny to see Esther but not beyond.

"Don't let—" he whispers.

"Too late. She's already seen it."

You remember Esther, yes? Daughter of Red Hot Fanny? Gentle voice? Come, come, if she were still a baby, how could she open a door? She's twelve now, almost thirteen, and the dark tuft of hair on her *keppie* reaches the middle of her back. At this very minute her long hair is not flowing. It's twisted and looped and fastened with a pencil in such a way that it doesn't fall into her eyes. Like a shield, she grasps a prayer book to her heart. Her shoulders and the corners of her mouth droop. Benny wishes he could have gotten to her before Fanny saw the announcement. He mouths, *I'm sorry*, but she just shrugs, defeated.

"Can I come in? Is Fanny decent?"

"Benny, darling. I'm never decent. That's why they call me Red Hot."

Esther looks to the heavens and shakes her head. "Mother, please. Close your robe."

Fanny tightens the belt on her sage-colored silk robe, hiding the tiny, feathered costume underneath. "You sure didn't get your modesty from me," she says, which just gets another eye roll from Esther.

"Come in, Benny." Esther opens the door wider.

"Put that book away, Esther dear, it's almost showtime," Fanny says. "Come, help me with my hair."

Esther carefully kisses the spine of the holy book she's been reading and puts it on the high shelf above a turquoise settee. It's the one spot in her mother's dressing room that isn't piled with pink tulle or red sequins or hats or makeup or perfume or brushes. It is the one place in Red Hot Fanny's dressing room that belongs to Esther.

Standing behind her mother, Esther arranges Fanny's copper curls with bobby pins. Benny folds the newspaper into a rectangle and puts it under his *tuchus* as he sits on the settee.

"Of course I already saw the announcement, Benjamin," Fanny says. She turns her head left and right, surveying her makeup and hair, and clips a rhinestone barrette at her right temple. "It sounds like an amazing opportunity for my Esther."

"Mother, I really would rather not." Esther is tired before this conversation starts, and there's a tightening at her throat as if all the things she wants to say are stuck there.

"At first, I thought, Well, this is nothing special. Every year Scheinfeld's has a Thursday night end-of-summer showcase."

"That's true," Benny says, perking up. He nods at Esther to say something.

Esther gazes into her mother's eyes in the mirror and clears her throat to say again what she's already said a million times. "That's right, Mother. I could skip this one, and study instead."

"But then I read on. *This* year's Thursday-night-end-of-summer showcase features Nicky Sanders. You know who that is, don't you?" She blows on her bright red nails and lifts her chin toward the newspaper folded on her vanity. "Read it for me, Esther."

Esther puts down the bobby pins and picks up the newspaper as if it might bite. "*Nicky Sanders Comes to Idylldale.* In honor of its thirty-sixth year, Scheinfeld's Resort and Cottages celebrates with a visit from Nicky Sanders. The comedy and theatrical genius—"

"Well, that's going a bit far," Fanny interrupts, blowing on her nails.

"*Theatrical genius*," Esther continues, "will perform, sign copies of his new book *Keep 'Em Laughing*, and judge a summer talent show."

"Not just any talent show," Fanny prompts.

"Okay . . ." Esther keeps her voice as bland as a sandwich without mustard. "All children under thirteen years of age are welcome to enter." She stops reading.

"Aren't you lucky, darling. You won't be thirteen until after the show!"

Esther's body feels like a bicycle tire that just ran over a tack. She wishes Benny could save her from the pain of this announcement, but he clearly tried. He probably came as soon as the paper arrived at Scheinfeld's. He probably jumped on the next trolley and rode all the way across town to the Heights to save Esther from the inevitable pressure to perform. If only Benny had known that Levi hand delivered the *Idylldale Inquirer* to Fanny's dressing room each afternoon so that she never misses a review or the latest scoop from the theater world.

"Honestly, *bubbele*, for someone raised in the theater, you aren't reading with feeling at all." Fanny extends her hand and Esther deposits the newspaper in her palm. She hums a scale, clears her throat, and says, "Project from the diaphragm, my love. And enunciate. Like this." Fanny reads the article as if it were a script for a Hollywood film. "The top five children's acts in the talent show will be featured on the *Nicky Sanders Show* to be broadcast live from Scheinfeld's Resort in Idylldale! And the winner of the show will receive"—Fanny pauses for effect—"one thousand dollars!"

Benny raises his eyebrows at Esther. That kind of money is no small potatoes. But Esther is watching her mother in the mirror they both face. It's framed with lights to show Fanny where she might need to add some rouge to cheer up her cheeks, or layer on mascara to make her eyes pop, or put more powder to hide the shine. But right now, she doesn't need rouge or mascara, because her cheeks are rosy with excitement and her eyes nearly pop out of her head. No powder can dim her inner glow when she says, just as Esther expects, "Essie. You simply must audition."

Esther follows Benny out of Fanny's dressing room and stands in the middle of the stage. "You simply must audition," she enunciates and projects from the diaphragm into the empty theater, sounding just like her mother.

Benny jumps off the stage and into the aisle below. "That's a pretty good imitation for someone who hates the theater."

"It's not that I *hate* it, Benny. It's just her dreams aren't my dreams."

"You know you don't have to explain it to me." Benny grimaces, picks up the newspaper, and shoves it in his back pocket. "I'm sorry I didn't get to you sooner."

"It's okay. She would have heard about the contest eventually." Esther slides off the stage and sits in row M—*M* for one of the few things she knows about her father, his name, Melvin. "Thanks for trying, Benny."

Benny squats in the aisle next to her seat. His hand pauses above her back. He pats twice, the same way he pats a taxi that's full of guests ready to leave Scheinfeld's. "I know you don't want to hear this, but you have a decent voice, Essie. And that kind of money is nothing to turn your back on. It might be a good opportunity?"

"A good opportunity for what exactly? A life of singing tawdry songs to an audience of the crass and faithless."

"Yikes. That's harsh, don't you think? Fanny, and the other actors, they're craftspeople."

"Ben, you're not listening. Singing about a monkey's *tuchus* isn't my idea of high art."

Benny laughs. "I love that one. It's so funny. His butt is red and he shakes it north, south, east, and west . . ."

Esther glares at Benny, and he stops shaking his own *tuchus*. "You've made my point."

"*My* point is that making people laugh *is* important."

"Important to you. And that's fine. But *I* want to raise my voice to God . . ."

They both finish, "On the *bima*."

"You may have mentioned that once or twice," Benny says. "But Esther, Rabbi Epstein doesn't even know you exist."

"I know." Esther bites on her thumbnail, thinking about the two birthday candles she'd saved long ago. On Fridays, when Fanny was out or getting notes on past performances, Esther would poke the birthday candles through the bottom of an egg carton and light them to celebrate Shabbos. Spying on the women in nearby apartments for guidance, she'd beckon the warmth toward her and let her hands rest over her eyes as they did. Then she'd pretend to pray—wishing she knew the real Hebrew. And for that moment, she felt more herself than any time Fanny put her on the stage. With her eyes closed and covered and the candle fire on the back of her hands, she breathed the burning beeswax and felt connected to every other person in Idylldale celebrating the Sabbath. Maybe even her far-away father was lighting candles at the same time. At the end of her murmurings, when she said amen and opened her eyes, she felt whole.

Over the years, the more she read, the more questions she had: Why was eating from the tree of knowledge a bad thing? Who was Mrs. Noah? And who was the first to step into the parted Red Sea?

But neither Fanny nor Millie, the costumer, were interested in questions about Torah.

"Look, kiddo," Levi said when she tried asking him. "*Shlemiels* like me, from the other side of the tracks, we don't ask those kinds of questions. We do what we're told. What you need is a rabbi."

Esther dreamed of a rabbi who would encourage her questions and care about her ideas. Someone like Rabbi Epstein who led the synagogue on the top of the hill near

Scheinfeld's. If he knew how much she wanted to learn, certainly he would want to teach her.

She shakes her head to clear her thoughts. "Benny, I know the Yiddish shows are part of my history and part of Idylldale. And for Mother, the theater *is* a kind of worship. But for me, something's missing. A way of thinking about ideas, understanding this . . . life! I know if I could study Torah, that I'd be more . . . more me. And look at me, almost thirteen, but in all twelve years Fanny's never let me learn Hebrew or even take the trolley alone up the hill to the synagogue . . ."

Esther's dreams swirl around the empty theater, sparkle in the ceiling mural clouds, and swoosh out the doors. All the trolley riders cock their heads and close their eyes as Esther's dream circles the brass bell so it vibrates and sings. When they open their eyes again, their vision is flooded with their deepest desires.

Back in the theater, Benny offers his hand and pulls Esther to standing. "What's this?" He points at the spot below her neck. When she looks down, he chucks her chin.

She slaps his hand. "Ben! Were you even listening?"

"Of course! But, Ess, now you need to listen to me. Sometimes you can't wait for permission to follow your dreams."

"Ben, you make it sound so easy. I can't just break rules like that. That's not me, either."

Benny cups his ear as he backs up the aisle. "Whatdya say? I gotta *shlep* bags for rich people."

"I said, you're not listening!" Esther calls, but now she's laughing.

"Nope. Can't hear ya." He taps his own head. "Is this thing on?"

Esther might as well be onstage—in the dark.

CHAPTER TWO

ROSE MORGENSTERN

SALT. IF YOU PUT too much of it in your matzo ball soup, people wince and stick out their tongues. Not enough, and uck! Bland, bland, bland. If you get the amount of salt just right, no one knows it's there. This is what Shira's life is like as the Rabbi's Daughter. She is supposed to be equal parts seen and invisible. Everyone in Idylldale knows Rabbi Epstein. They admire his quiet, commanding way and his steady, thoughtful words. So when Shira is recognized as "The Rabbi's Daughter," she has to be very careful about what she says and how she acts.

Unfortunately for Shira, in life and in soup, she likes a lot more salt than the rabbi.

Visiting sick and dying people in the hospital is the thing she hates most about being the Rabbi's Daughter. For the longest time Shira had short hair, and when she would visit the patients, some of whom were a little loopy, they would address her as *yingele*, or *little boy*. She grew her hair to her shoulders so she'd no longer have that problem. Then, there is the hospital smell—a *bisl* ammonia, a *bisl* puke. Shira used to hold her breath so she wouldn't smell it. But the saddest thing you might remember is that her very own mother died in this exact hospital twelve years and forty-nine weeks ago.

These things make the hospital a troublesome place for Shira, but she does love visiting their first patient—Rose Morgenstern. Rose never thinks that Shira is too-much-salt.

Rabbi Epstein knocks on Rose's door. *Mayne kinder.* Do you remember when Benny Bell knocked on Red Hot Fanny's dressing room door looking for Esther? That four-knuckle knock said *Quick! Let me in! I've got news!* Well, Rabbi Epstein has perfected the one-knuckle quiet knock for his hospital visits. The one-knuckle knock is feathery soft and says *I'm here now, so if you don't mind, and I'm not intruding, then maybe I could come in? I wouldn't want to be any trouble.*

"Come in, Rabbi," says Mrs. Morgenstern, who is well acquainted with the rabbi's knock.

"Rose. How are you feeling?" Rabbi Epstein sits in the extra chair beside Mrs. Morgenstern's bed and gently holds one of her weak and spindly hands.

"I can't complain," Mrs. Morgenstern tells them. "The bad news is the food here is terrible. The good news is I don't have to cook."

Shira laughs out loud, and Rabbi Epstein gives her a too-much-salt look. She sees this look a lot.

"Rose, what do the tests show? What does the doctor say?"

"They're still looking at the test results. The doctor says whatever is wrong with my lungs won't kill my sense of humor." Her joke lands and Shira smiles. "Who decides on the heat in here anyway? *Oy vey*. First, I'm cold. Then I'm hot. It's so dry in here . . ."

"How dry is it?" Shira says slyly.

No doubt you have a good sense of humor and you're no stranger to classic joke setups. There's the *knock-knock* setup, the *what's-the-deal-with* setup, and the *did-you-hear-about-the-one* setup, but one of the essential, all-time joke setups is the *fake-question-begging-to-be-answered* setup. Too bad

Rabbi gives Shira another too-much-salt look and pats Rose's hand. "I'll get you some water."

"Yes, please, Rabbi." Mrs. Morgenstern winks at Shira as he leaves the room.

"How dry is it?" Shira says with a giggle.

"So dry, people are bringing me cactuses instead of flowers." The two of them burst out into giggles. "*Nu?* What joke have you got for me today, funny Shira?"

Shira considers the bedside chair, but the papery thinness of Mrs. Morgenstern's skin shows too many veins for Shira to hold her hand, so she stays standing. Better for performing, anyway. "So, there's a man who goes to a tailor, and the tailor gives him a suit. And the man says, 'But the left leg is too long.'

"'Not if you stick out your leg a bit,' says the tailor." Shira sticks out her leg.

"And the man says, 'But the right arm is too short.'

"And the tailor says, 'Pull your elbow into your body a bit.'" Shira pretends to be the man twisting his body to make the suit look right.

Mrs. Morgenstern chuckles, because Shira is hamming it up as the oddly shaped man and also because, as a school principal for many years, she has heard this joke a million times.

"So the man buys the suit and walks down the street," Shira continues. "And two women see him. The one says, 'That poor man.'

"And the other says, 'But what a fine-looking suit.'"

Now Mrs. Morgenstern lets out a gigantic laugh. There's no better sound to a performer's ears. "Oh, what would I do without your jokes, Shira?" Then her face grows serious, and she throws a glance at the door. "Is he coming?"

Shira looks down the hall. Rabbi Epstein is talking with the nurses at their station. "No."

"Then here, this is just for you. I took it from the corkboard in the hall." Rose reaches under her pillow and pulls out a torn piece of newspaper folded in fourths. When Shira tries to take it, Rose holds on, and Shira can't pull it away. The hand that looked so frail is stronger than she thought it would be, and the paper is trapped in the middle. Rose brings their hands to her lips and plants a kiss on Shira's knuckles. "My Ellen, may she rest in peace, used to say, *Az me est khazer, zol rinen fun bord!* Be yourself, dear Shira, remember that."

Rabbi Epstein enters and Rose lets go. "Here's fresh water."

Shira turns away and catches a glimpse of the folded news article as she slides it into her pocket. The headline— NICKY SANDERS COMES TO IDYLLDALE.

She's still thinking about Mrs. Morgenstern's Yiddish proverb. *If you're going to do something wrong, enjoy it!*

Mayne kinder, what wrong thing is Shira going to do?

CHAPTER THREE

ASKED AND ANSWERED

SHIRA COULD HARDLY BELIEVE that Nicky Sanders was going to be in Idylldale. And more than that, the auditions would be at Scheinfeld's Resort and Cottages, steps away from her father's synagogue. But parent persuasion can be as sticky as challah dough. Shira prefers the ask-over-and-over method combined with puppy eyes and love. Esther prefers reasoned arguments. I have found that people are most agreeable when they have a full and happy tummy.

Perhaps Shira thinks so too, because as they clean up from the rabbi's favorite brisket dinner, she thinks it's the perfect time to do a little parent persuasion.

"It looks like Mrs. Applebaum is home from visiting her son in New York." Rabbi Epstein leans toward the window above the kitchen sink.

"I wonder if they saw a Broadway show?"

"If they did, I'm sure she'll tell you all about it," he says, looking at their own lawn. "It might be time to mow the grass."

"Did you hear about the sad lawn mower?"

"Shira."

"He hit a rough patch." Shira does a time step from her long-ago tap dance lessons and spins. "Ta-da."

"Very good." He pats her shoulder. "Enough."

Shira wilts like old lettuce. This isn't going to be easy. "Let's watch *Nicky Sanders*, Papa!" Shira leads him to their couch, opens the television cabinet, and turns the dial. With a *click* and a *pop*, the star in the middle of the screen grows into the black-and-white picture of a Nibbles potato chip bag.

Shira snuggles under her father's outstretched arm. But she can't hold back the first few bars of the potato chip jingle. "*Because we've got no quibbles with the crispy, crunchy, always need to munch a chiiip caaalled Nibbles.*"

"Hush, Shira. Just listen."

Shira crosses her arms and presses her lips together hard. She listens as Nicky Sanders gives his monologue and Rabbi Epstein laughs in all the right places. How come it's okay for Nicky Sanders to tell jokes but not Shira?

Next, the studio band plays and two people waltz. The lights in the television studio sparkle off the crystals in the woman's skirt, and Shira can't help but think of her eighth birthday when her father let her take dance lessons.

The dance captain at Scheinfeld's Resort and Cottages, a man who moved like sunlight on the Idylldale River, had taught her to tuck her derriere (which her father calls a *tuchus*) and to keep her upper body tight but not stiff. She learned the waltz and the foxtrot with a boy from New York City. Together they *one, two, three*–ed and *slow, slow, quick, quick*–ed until she felt like she was flying. When they performed at the gazebo, the rabbi caught it all on his movie camera. He stored that film in the back of his closet with a box of her mother's keepsakes. But you can't store passion like a film canister. Had she been good enough to be on the *Nicky Sanders Show* then?

Her papa's full and happy belly isn't going to last for-ever. Shira puts her hand in her pocket, and the paper that Mrs. Morgenstern gave her strengthens her resolve. "Papa, wouldn't it be great if I were on this show?"

He peels his eyes from the screen to glance at her. "*This* show? On the television? That wouldn't happen, Shirala. Adults are on that show."

"What if I told you that Nicky Sanders is going to have a children's talent show?"

"I'd say good luck to all the children in New York City."

"Yes! Normally, yes! But, holy casserole, Papa, Nicky Sanders is coming here! To audition children in Idylldale!"

"You didn't let me finish." He looks at her long and hard. "Good luck to the children in New York City *whose parents don't know how to set boundaries*."

Shira was used to these declarations from her father and rarely let them stop her. "But Papa, remember when I took dance lessons?"

"Shira. Not this again."

"I'm just saying, I'd love to audition."

"Ah, Shirala is *just-saying*. You're always *just-saying* some-thing about performing, so you already know what I'm going to *just-say*. No. Now is the time to focus on your bat mitzvah. There's only two weeks to go. Do you feel ready, Shirala?"

Some people see the rabbi and think grizzly bear. Shira sees a teddy bear who can be loved into submission. "You're right, darling Papa." Shira says finally. "I have not put enough effort into studying."

"Oh, pshh." He rolls his eyes. "You're just saying what you think I want to hear. I will not be moved by those big green eyes, even though you are my one and only daughter. Hush now." On the TV, Nicky Sanders pretends to fight with a made-up neighbor about a fence.

"What if I work really hard on my Torah portion, and I'm really serious . . ."

The rabbi scoffs as if Shira has finally told a joke he finds funny. "You? Serious?"

She narrows her eyes at him. "I can be serious, Papa. If I can focus like you say, would you let me audition?" She clasps her hands together and kneels beside the couch. "It's Nicky Sanders!"

The rabbi rubs at his eyes a little and his fingers rest on the bridge of his nose. "When you were little, I was a father alone, and all the mothers were sending their children to ballet and tap dance class. You wanted tap, so, I sent you to tap. I thought it was what your mother would do."

He looks so sad when he mentions her mother that Shira climbs up on the couch with him and kisses the top of his head. "You are a wonderful papa."

"And you are a wonderful daughter, but now that you're older, you'll focus on your studies. It's time to be responsible."

"And yet . . ." She hugs him, squeezing her eyes closed against the *no* she's about to get. "I bet Mama would want me to audition for a show."

Rabbi Epstein releases her and holds his head in his hands. At the synagogue, he is the rabbi. There, the Torah and the Talmud tell him how to live. At home, he is Papa, the only parent to a very persistent girl. Living is never as clear as his books suggest it should be. Following a recipe, it isn't. "No, Shira," he says. "She would not."

"But . . ."

"You asked. I answered. No." Just like a grizzly, he looks more intimidating standing up. "The theater is a bastion of impropriety," he says, and leaves Shira on the couch feeling as flat as a potato latke. Nicky Sanders sings his goodbye song.

When she hears her father's door close, she points into the air and whispers her imitation. "A bastion of impropriety." Shira folds her arms and hugs her dreams closer. "I'll just have to find another way."

⁓

They say *waste not, want not.* Esther and Fanny don't have much to waste, but it doesn't keep them from wanting. Their single room on the fourth floor of a brownstone has a bed, a changing screen, a dresser, a refrigerator, a sink, a small tub hidden under the kitchen counter, a hot plate for cooking, a little table, and a couple of chairs. Since the room is so small, they've had to choreograph their bedtime routines so they don't run into each other. It always starts the same.

"Go to the toilet before Mr. Silverman from 3B stinks it up," Fanny says. "Or Joshua and Minna's little *pishers* miss the bowl."

"Mother," Esther admonishes as always. Still, she peeks into the hallway to confirm that the toilet door is open, and when she's done, she heads back to their room, passing Fanny on the way. She washes, changes quickly, jumps up onto the bed, and turns on the bedside lamp before Fanny returns.

Fanny's hand hovers over the wall switch. "Ready?"

"Ready."

Esther never tires of watching her mother's routines. Fanny disappears behind the changing screen. Carved and lacquered Japanese cherry branches reach gracefully across its three panels. "Tell me again where the screen came from, Mother."

"It was a gift from a playwright who couldn't pay the theater after we'd put on his show." She emerges from the screen partition pinning her hair in a twist.

"And that silk gown?"

She leans close to Esther and makes a silly face. "From a secret admirer," she says with a Russian accent.

"And what did my father give you?"

Fanny's face falls for a tiny moment before her smile reappears. She bops Esther's nose with her finger. "Mel gave me you, and it was the greatest gift of all." She kisses Esther's forehead and moves on to the rest of her routine. She wraps her hair in a scarf and uncaps the Noxzema. The eucalyptus-scented face cream is bittersweet and stringent, and it burns Esther's nostrils. Fanny rubs, wipes, and rinses. One moment she is Red Hot Fanny rouged for the stage, the next she is just Esther's mother.

"There you are," Esther says, as she always does. Fanny smiles and slides next to Esther between the sheet and blanket, and Esther clicks off the light. She thinks of the religious stories of her namesake and how *that* Esther had to act without asking permission—just like Benny said. She inhales to fortify herself and says, "Mama. Do you remember the first time I was onstage?"

"The first time you were on the stage, my darling, you were a baby wrapped in a bundle of linen. You played a baby in Chelm."

"Did I like it?"

"Well, you cried a lot. I had to pass you, all bundled up, to Millie, and she handed me a doll instead. The doll was quiet."

"And then?"

"And then . . ." Fanny taps her chin, thinking back through the many shows she's done. "Well, from then on, my love, every show was the same. Millie and I dressed you in all sorts of costumes for all sorts of roles, but you know what you always did?"

"Found a book and read in a corner."

"Exactly. You are my book girl. Too smart for the Idylldale schools."

What is it about mamas thinking their children are the best thing since sliced bread? Now, sliced bread! That's something to marvel at.

"You have a fabulous memory," Fanny went on. "It's such a shame it's not being put to better use! You're amazing as an understudy, but imagine if a director saw your memorization skills. There'd be no end to your work!"

"But I go onstage because you need me. Never because I want it." It's the first time Esther has said it quite so plain.

The other side of the bed is silent. And silent some more. Esther looks over and sees that Fanny is still awake. "Nicky Sanders, he . . ." Fanny seems mesmerized by the stripes of light that snake between the horizontal blinds and stretch across the wall. Finally, she shakes as if she's getting rid of the thoughts beneath her head scarf. "Nicky Sanders could make you famous." Fanny pats Esther's hand. "The stage may not be your first love, but you need to audition."

Esther stares at the same stripes of light. She wants to say, *You want to be famous—not me.* But instead she says, "Mother, all the evidence is clear."

"Ha!" Fanny's short laugh fills the small room. "What's the evidence, *bubbele?*"

"One. You know I've never loved the theater. That's your thing." Fanny opens her mouth, but Esther stops her with an open hand. "Two. I've always loved books and study. Three . . ." She takes a deep breath and hurries through, "The time would be much better spent studying Torah with the rabbi."

"*Oy,* again with the rabbi?" Fanny turns and props herself on her elbow. "Esther, any other child would give their right arm to be on the stage."

"If you'd just let me meet him. Let me go to the synagogue. What's the harm?" Esther props on her elbow. They are eye to eye. Rosenbaum to Rosenbaum. That's a lot of steadfastness.

A car goes by.

"I need you to audition for Nicky Sanders," Fanny says, and there's something in her eyes that is more serious than Esther has ever seen. "I'll let you pick the song. No 'Monkey's Tuchus.' I know you hate that one." She murmurs to herself, "It wouldn't win the contest anyway."

Esther is done presenting her case. She wants to say, *Give me one good reason that I can't study.* Or, *Why don't you understand that this is important to me?* Or, *What have you got against Torah study?* She wishes she had her own room with a door she could slam. But she has to make do with what she has. She rolls over with a huff and scooches to the edge of the bed—as far away from her mother as she can possibly get.

Her mother's breath gets deeper and slower. Esther thinks Fanny is asleep until she says, "You know . . . the Yiddish theater is part of your Jewish culture too. You don't have to love the stage, but maybe you could try to like it a little, eh?"

Fanny reaches out to stroke Esther's hair and sings.

A bisl zun (a bit of rain)

A bisl regn (a bit of sun)

A ruik ort dem kop tsu leygn (a quiet place to lay your head)

Abi gezunt, ken men gliklekh zayn (as long as you're well, you can be happy)

On all other nights, this song calms Esther, like her own special lullaby. On all other nights she appreciates the love she has in her little apartment with her mother, and she falls straight to sleep. Tonight is different. Tonight, she tosses and turns as longing smolders low in her belly.

On one side of town, Esther wants to study at the synagogue on the hill. On the other side, Shira wants to be onstage.

In between the two girls, the trolley bell clangs.

CHAPTER FOUR

THE TROLLEY

AT THE DELI, MOST people know exactly what they want. They stride to the counter and say, "Morty, gimme a pastrami on rye with mustard." Bing, bang, boom. I make it, wrap it up, and off they go. Other customers stare at the menu forever. I got all day, so I don't mind, but at the theater, later in the week, Esther still hasn't chosen a song, and Fanny's jaw is clenched so tight she wouldn't be able to eat my pastrami, on rye or anything else.

"If one cannot decide on a song," she says, "it is hard for one to rehearse."

"I just don't like the ones you've chosen. They're too . . . too . . ."

"Too *grown-up*," Benny says carefully.

Esther extends her arm to Benny in the orchestra seats. "Yes. Too grown-up." She twists her hair and secures it with a pencil on the back of her head.

"You can do grown-up. You're the daughter of Red Hot Fanny."

"As we've discussed, Mother, I'm your *daughter*. Not you."

"Kid acts are hard, Frances," Millie says.

"We'll find the right song," says Joshua at the piano.

Fanny throws her hands to the sky. "Take five," she says and exits with a swirl of her shawl.

Esther slides off the stage and into the seat next to Benny. "Boy, oh boy, has it been a week."

"I don't get it. Why does she want you to audition so badly?"

Esther sighs. "I have no idea, but I wish someone else could do it for me." She grabs his shirt, yanking and pushing. Benny flops back and forth under her grasp, like a rag doll. "That's it, Ben. You can put on a dress and be me."

"If I did that, Nicky Sanders would definitely choose me for the show!" Benny winks at her. "But no one's gonna believe I'm you."

"I know." Esther falls back in her seat. "What am I going to do?"

"I don't know what you're going to do. But if I'm not at my post on time, Miss Scheinfeld yells." He shudders, and the two of them rock to their feet. At the street corner, Benny puts his hands on her shoulders. "It's gonna be okay, Ess. I'll put my thinking cap on." Then he waves his red cap and hustles to the Trolley Transfer Station.

Approaching midtown Idylldale, Benny checks the pocket watch he got from the hotel lost and found. Sunday is a big day at Scheinfeld's. In the morning, guests from the previous week check out, and in the afternoon, new guests check in with their bins, bags, and boxes. He has to be there at noon for all of it, and he's cutting it close. There goes his trolley now! Benny bangs on the back of the trolley car to stop the driver from pulling away. As it slows, he grabs a pole and swings aboard.

Like the fancy men and women in slick suits, he intends to hold on to the ceiling strap. But when the trolley bumps and the looped leather straps sway, his fingertips brush and miss their target, and he flies down the aisle, arms flailing.

He dodges a woman with a baby in one arm and groceries in the other. Luckily, he catches a second pole that keeps him from landing in the lap of a laughing girl—a girl, oddly, whose dark hair is twisted and secured with a pencil.

Wait. He just left Esther. How could she be here on the trolley? He looks. And looks again. But unlike Esther's giggle, this girl's laughter stings a little, like salt in a wound. "What's so funny?" His words stab at her laughter.

"Your arms and body looked like spaghetti!" the girl blurts, without any of Esther's usual reserve. "It was hilarious! You even crossed your eyes. Work *that* into an act for Nicky Sanders." She sticks out her hand. "I'm Shira. And you are?"

Even though the girl says her name is Shira, Benny still has to blink when she removes the pencil and her hair tumbles to her shoulders. She has the identical brown ringlets in her hair, smooth olive skin, and slight bump at the top of her nose that Esther has. This Shira even has the pine-needle-green eyes that he's noticed on more than one occasion when he's been with Esther.

But this girl, this Shira girl, is wearing pants like a sailor would wear, with two sets of buttons—not a skirt like Esther wears. She speaks with the brashness of a sailor too, and has no star-shaped mole on her neck. She isn't Esther, but she could have fooled him.

"You could take a photograph, it would last longer," Shira says and gives Benny's shoulder a little chuck.

Benny, realizing he's been staring, sputters a bit. "S-sorry. I'm Ben. Benny Bell. Are you auditioning for the Sanders show?" The trolley lurches, and Benny and the other standing passengers sway and grip their poles. The man next to Shira gets off. Benny sits.

Was she going to audition? Shira thinks of her father's definite *no*. She leans in with a conspiratorial whisper. "You don't go to synagogue, do you."

"Um . . . Not recently." Benny blushes and clears his throat. "Things are busy with my family and at Scheinfeld's and . . . Hey. What do you care for, anyway?"

Shira hasn't yet mentioned that she is Shira-the-Rabbi's-Daughter. Benny's banter is making her laugh, and most kids stiffen when they find out who her father is. She'd rather he just gets to know her a little first, the way you get to know the butcher before you buy his brisket, so she ignores his question. "You work at Scheinfeld's? I'm there from time to time with my father. Bellhop?"

"*Senior* bellhop. I'm allowed to talk on the two-way radio."

"Excuse me. *Senior* bellhop. And your name is Benny Bell?" She holds in a laugh and snorts instead.

"Well, it's more of a stage name. *Benjamin Zuckerman* just doesn't have the right ring."

"Ring. Bell." Now Shira lets herself laugh and nudges his shoulder with her own. "That's good. Put that in the act too."

"You think I'm funny?"

"Sure I do. And I should know. I love the stage."

"Well, thanks. Not everyone agrees."

"Oh yeah? Like who? You want I should break his knees?"

Benny scoffs. "Well, Levi, for one, but he's the *shtarker* at the Heights, so I don't know if you're tough enough." He winks.

"You mean the Heights, the theater? You've been there?"

"All the time."

"I've never been," she sighs.

"You love the stage and you've never been to the Heights?" Benny clutches his cap to his heart in disbelief.

"All right, all right." She sighs wistfully. "I want to go, but the only performances I've seen have been children's shows at Scheinfeld's, or on TV."

"TV's not the same as the Yiddish theater."

"No. I imagine not. But other than in Idylldale, hardly anyone speaks Yiddish now."

She scratches at the base of her neck and shoulders where it tickles. Benny notices that her hair isn't quite as long as Esther's.

"Anyway, you're very funny for a *senior bellhop*. Sort of in a *junior comedian* way," she says, nudging Benny again.

The trolley crosses the bridge and starts up the hill through the medium-size houses toward Scheinfeld's.

"So, *do* you have an act?" Benny asks again.

"No. My father won't let me audition. He hates that I want to perform. He wants me to *raise my voice to God*."

Benny stiffens. Weren't those the same words Esther used?

"I know. He's very serious about it."

"Your father must be a very pious man."

"Oh, the most pious." Shira pauses a bit before she delivers the news. "He's . . . well, he's Rabbi Epstein." Just as Shira predicted, Benny squirms a bit and gives her a little more space despite the crowded trolley. But as they say, *suspense is worse than the ordeal itself,* so she tells him everything. "Even though I'm his kid, I'm a little like the *rebbetzin,* because my mother died when I was born. Like today! We just finished visiting the hospital and he's off to a community meeting, so I'm in charge of dinner and groceries, and I still have to study for my bat mitzvah." She shakes her head. "My father has a very specific path he wants me to follow."

"And it's not a path you'd choose?"

"If it weren't for my dad, I'd try out for Nicky Sanders in two shakes of the monkey's *tuchus.* But one must obey one's parents. At least that's what I'm told." The trolley bell rings as they cross the river. "Benny Bell, have you ever wanted something so badly, but your life took you in the exact opposite direction?"

"Well, not me, but actually . . ."

"I mean, all my life I've wanted to sing, dance, tell jokes, but it's always"—she straightens up, wags her finger, and lowers her voice—"*Shira, it's time to study Torah. Shira, you've been raised in the synagogue, you should know this. Your Hebrew*

pronunciation is atrocious. Shira, you have to be more serious."
She throws her hands in the air, then notices where she is on
the hillside and pulls the stop request cord. "That was a lot,
I guess. I have a habit of going overboard."

Benny can't help but wonder if the trolley floor magically
buckled and gave him a little push toward Shira to set this
all in motion. "Shira Epstein," he says with a sneaky grin, "I
have someone I'd like you to meet."

CHAPTER FIVE

A MIRROR IMAGE

SOMETIMES, IT'S HARD TO shake a thought. Me, I try to keep my mind empty at the deli. If I don't, I could burn myself on an oven or slice my thumb instead of the corned beef.

All through his shift at Scheinfeld's last night, Benny'd been thinking about Shira and Esther. Not only were they almost identical, but also ... they each wanted what the other had. When he stumbled from Scheinfeld's Eastern Idylldale Trolley line (the EIT) to the textile mill's Western Idylldale Trolley line (the WIT) at the Trolley Transfer Station, he knew the perfect place for them to meet the next day.

"Just when Fanny gives me a break to read, you say I have to *come on*? I don't understand what the big deal is, Ben."

"You'll see."

Benny and Esther pass the spires and arches of the Idylldale Public Library, and it's all he can do to keep her from detouring to the bookshelves. "Not now," he says, and tugs her wrist. "We're meeting someone."

"Someone whom?"

"Come on, Esther," Benny says, walking so fast Esther jogs to keep up. She swerves through delivery men who call out morning greetings to one another. Car engines chug and gears grind. The smell of morning bread wafts from a bakery across the cobblestones to meet them.

Arriving at the station, Benny stops short, and Esther runs right into his back with an "*Oof!*"

He takes her by the shoulders. "Now listen, Ess. What'd you tell me in the theater the other day? What do you tell me all. The. Time?"

Esther scrutinizes his face, trying to determine what he's *really* asking. "That I don't want to sing about the monkey's *tuchus*?"

"Ha. Well yeah, that." Benny chuckles. "I mean what else. About raising your voice?"

"To God. On the *bima*. To be a bat mitzvah?" Esther gasps. "Are you taking me to the synagogue? Ben. You know I'm not allowed."

"No, not exactly." Benny moves her out of the way as a telegram delivery boy on a bicycle zips by, his bell *ting-ting-*ing as he passes. "Look. I don't know why Torah is better to you than the roar of the crowd or the shine of the spotlight, but you're my friend. So go *there*." He turns her so that she faces the Trolley Transfer Station. "That's where you'll meet her and find the answer you're looking for. And once you do, come find me." With that, he jumps aboard the outbound EIT, just pulling up to the station.

"Benjamin! That's where I meet who?" she calls, but he's off to Scheinfeld's once again. "I mean 'whom.' And what answer?" She throws her hands up and lets them fall. "I don't even know the question."

She ducks under the copper-covered roof that wraps around the squat, round brick building and walks around the outside of the station, feeling like she's on a carousel. The trolleys come and go—inbound, outbound, east, west.

One group of riders disembarks and another group gets on. Some riders wait on benches. Others slip inside to buy a cup of coffee, the paper, or use the bathroom. With their tokens and packages, babies and briefcases, they are almost interchangeable. The trolleys *click clack* from one track to another. *Time to go home*, Esther thinks.

Just then, a trolley pulls away from the station and reveals a girl. Looking at this girl is like Esther looking in a mirror.

"Holy casserole," the girl says. "We do look alike! I'm Shira. Benny thought we should meet."

Esther's mouth is set in a shocked *O*. "Oh . . . dear . . . God," she says, and the clang of the trolley bell vibrates through the station.

CHAPTER SIX

A SWEET TRIP

THE TWO GIRLS CIRCLE each other, taking in the enormity of the situation. *Mayne kinder.* They are a little suspicious, maybe cautious, yes? It's as if they've each found a long-lost sister, but you and I know that can't be. Even though they look similar and share a birthday, they have a different mother and father. They are not twins; that we know. The girls soon know this too. Bewildered, trying to find the common thread, they run through the important details: their names, their family names, their ages.

"Okay, so, definitely not secret sisters. But, we're birthday twins?!" Shira hears herself squealing, but she can't help it. "That is just bananas. Plus, our birthday is around the corner, and it's a big one, right? Thirteen! Time for my father to ease up a little, if you ask me. Your dad can't possibly be stricter?"

Esther, overwhelmed by Shira's exuberance and not eager to say anything about her missing father, is stunned silent.

"Okay, touchy subject? Esther? What about your dad? Or mom? Something? Anything? Um . . . Your favorite birthday present?"

Esther's favorite gift is on the tip of her tongue, but she's unsure about sharing this too.

"Come on, I won't laugh."

"Fine. A secondhand *siddur* with gold accents on the inside. Levi got it for me last year."

Shira doesn't laugh at all, but she also doesn't say that her world is full of free *siddurs*. Prayer books to hand out at the beginning of services, prayer books to collect for careful storage, prayer books to kiss on the spine if she drops one. Okay, so they don't share a common taste in gifts. She doesn't press the point. Instead she says, "Is that the Levi at the Heights Benny was talking about? The *shtarker*?"

"Levi, a *shtarker*? He can calm a rowdy audience just with his eyes, yes, but he also does lights at the Heights."

"Wait. How do *you* know so much about the Heights?"

"Well, because the Heights is . . . home. I learned to sew from Millie, the costume mistress. Joshua, the accompanist, taught me to read music. And my mother . . ." She looks to the heavens and sighs. "Is Red Hot Fanny."

"Are you kidding!" Shira shoves Esther playfully on the shoulder. "I would give anything to see her in a show. You didn't ask, but *my* favorite present was a pair of tap shoes I got when I was eight. Of course, I outgrew them, but I still have them in my closet."

"Huh. What do your parents do?"

"It's just my papa. Mama died."

"Oh. I'm sorry." Esther still doesn't mention that Fanny is all she has too.

"I was tiny. Too little to remember." Shira waves away the condolences and moves on. "My father is Rabbi Epstein."

Esther shakes her head in surprise. The man that she's wanted to meet for so long is this girl's father? This gets better and better. Shira has everything Esther wants. "That must be amazing. And intimidating! Living with such a learned man." Esther can't believe it. "So he's pretty strict?"

"Papa? Well, he's just a big teddy bear. But when he's mad, I know it. He does this thing where he glares at me over his nose—hawk eyes, I call it." She shudders. "That's when I wish I hadn't . . . that Mama were still here." A moment before, she had waved away her mother's absence as if it were unimportant, but now she has a lump in her throat. She leaves the bench abruptly.

"Hey," Esther says, reaching out a hand. "Are you okay?"

"It's just, sometimes, he tells me the story about when I was born. He says they put me on Mama's chest all wrapped in a blanket. He says she nursed me, that she gave me all her love, but the next morning . . ." Shira swallows hard. Who is this girl to make her feel these things all of a sudden? "Sure, I'm okay." She presses the heels of her hands into her eyes. When she turns back to Esther, the sadness is replaced by a practiced smile. "Candy?"

Esther pats her pockets. "I don't have any money."

"My treat. What's allowance for?" In the station, Shira picks out a pile of licorice whips and candy sticks striped like barber poles.

"Thanks," says Esther. "Do you come here with your friends a lot? My mother is strict like your father. I'd never have gotten here without Benny's help. The library is as far as I'm allowed to go."

Shira sighs and wraps the licorice thread around her finger. "Ah, friends. I've heard of those. But you know . . . Rabbi's Daughter."

Esther shakes her head. She has no idea. It seems like being friends with the Rabbi's Daughter would be such an honor.

"Other kids don't have to go to the hospital when someone they don't know is ill, or set prayer books on the pews, or stand next to their father after services and shake hands and know everyone's name. People think I'm a goody two-shoes."

Esther thinks of all the times that she's had to pay the rent or settle their tab at the local deli. Things that her father might have helped with if he were still around.

"What about you?" Shira counters. "You're theater royalty. Daughter of Red Hot Fanny!" She shakes her shoulders in a shimmy that makes Esther blush.

"Oh, stop that. Well . . . when I was smaller, Mother and Millie used to dress me up in Shirley Temple dresses and try to get me to do—"

"'Good Ship Lollipop'?"

Esther stops sucking on the candy with a *pop*. "Yes!"

"I loved that song!" Shira says at the same time Esther says, "I hated it!"

Esther pauses. "You loved it?"

"I performed that at my sixth birthday, and Papa filmed it on his Brownie camera. I remember realizing, somewhere in the middle, between the monkeys and the lions, that Papa was the only father at the party. It's happy and sad, you know? I was happy he was there, but I think that's when I realized what it meant not to have a mama." Shira watches the newsie, snipping twine from bundles of papers, and Esther watches Shira. In that moment Esther realizes that she and Shira not only look the same, they also share the same grief.

"Let's suck all the stripes off," Esther says, changing the subject away from Shira's sadness.

Shira tucks a loose hair behind Esther's ear. Somehow, it feels as if they've always shared these familiarities. "So what about your father?"

"I don't know much about him. Not even his last name. I have Fanny's—Rosenbaum. I know he was a traveling salesman who was in Idylldale less than a month. He and Fanny loved each other, 'body and soul,' or so she tells me. But Fanny's always made it very clear that my father wasn't coming back."

"Wowza," Shira says, and waggles her eyebrows. "If he loved her so much, I wonder why he left."

Esther stops swirling the candy on her tongue, bites her bottom lip, and looks directly at Shira. "Because of me, I think?"

"That. Can't. Be," Shira says, punctuating each word with a wag of her candy stick, then hands another licorice lace to Esther. "Do you know what kinds of things your father sold?"

"Encyclopedias. Mother says that's why I have a thirst for knowledge. I'd rather read than act any day." Esther swirls the candy on her tongue again, making the end into a sharp point. It's so much easier to say this to Shira than to Fanny— or anyone at the Heights. "But I've got a good memory, too good to waste, my mother says. So, I fill in for people a lot."

"You're an understudy? That's fantastic! You get to learn all the parts."

Esther shrugs, surprised that Shira makes this sound like a good thing. "Now she's making me audition for that stupid Nicky Sanders talent contest."

Shira claps her hands once, and the sound echoes around the station. A knot of pigeons flutter into the air, then peck again at a stale bagel on the ground. "That's what *I* really want—to audition for Nicky Sanders. Who, I'll have you know, is a comic genius. Instead, I have to study"—she mimics her father with a deep, slow voice and a stern look over her nose—"'*diligently*' for my bat mitzvah on my—our—birthday! And by then the audition—" Shira jumps from the bench, and the rest of her candy falls on the ground.

"Shira, your candy!"

"Esther! Forget about the candy!" Shira waggles her *tuchus* like the monkey in the song. "I know why Benny got us together! '*Az me est khazer, zol rinen fun bord!*'"

"'If you're going to do something wrong, enjoy it'?"

Shira puts her hands on Esther's shoulders. "Esther. You take my place at the bat mitzvah. I'll take your place at the audition. We'll each get what we want."

"Oh, Shira." Esther pockets the rest of her candy with finality and steps away. "That's ridiculous." Shira's hands slip from Esther's shoulders. Esther meets her own eyes in Shira's face, traces the bump in Shira's nose on her own, lets her shaky hand land on her star-shaped mole that keeps the two of them from being identical. Shira puts her hands together in prayer, and her eyebrows travel toward the heavens. "Nope.

Definitely no. This would never work." Esther turns sharply and walks away. "One: It would be crazy. Two: It would be *so* wrong. And three: Don't you think our parents will know who we are? I mean, they aren't stupid. Right?"

Shira jogs to catch up and stops in front of Esther. She knows right away that sad eyes and pleading won't win Esther over. Esther, she can see, appreciates facts. But parents? Well, she's noticed that they see what they want to see. If Shira can convince Esther, they have a chance at their dreams!

"Esther, wait. That Shirley Temple performance wasn't the only one. I used to sing popular songs for people all the time at the synagogue picnics. After I got the dancing shoes, Papa even got me lessons with the dance captain at Scheinfeld's. And then when I was ten, he cut me off. He said I was too old for that childishness anymore. All of a sudden it was *grocery store* this, and *learn how to cook* that." Shira takes a deep breath, and Esther can see their shared sadness at having to follow their parents' wishes instead of their own dreams. "Anyway. I *am* a good performer. I am a *great* performer. I can be you, audition for Nicky Sanders, and I bet . . . I bet I can even win. It'll be the role of a lifetime!"

Shira grabs Esther's shoulders. "And with your memory, you can learn the Torah portion. You'd be a much better Rabbi's Daughter than I ever could."

"You know . . ." Esther looks at their matching saddle shoes. "I'm going to tell you something that not even Benny knows." She looks back at Shira. "I have a couple of birthday candles that I use as Shabbos candles, but I don't know the prayers, so I just make stuff up."

"I can help you with that."

"If we do this, I'll finally get my chance to study Torah."

"And I'll get a chance to perform." Shira stretches out a hand.

Esther takes it.

Both of the girls are breathing as if they hiked all the way from the river valley to the synagogue at the top of the hill.

Who knew that deciding to disobey one's parents would be such hard work?

CHAPTER SEVEN

SNIP, SNIP

SHIRA MARCHES OVER TO the newsie, and Esther follows. "Can I borrow your scissors?"

"I can't give you these. My boss'll kill me," the boy says.

"What do you still have for candy, Ess?"

Esther holds out two candy sticks and two licorice whips.

"I'll give you these if we can use them. Promise. I'll bring 'em back." The newsie shrugs and hands her the scissors.

"Don't run with those," Esther cautions, and follows her into the bathroom.

Once they are both in front of the mirror, Shira grabs a small bunch of Esther's longer hair and tugs. "If you're gonna be me, some of this has got to go."

"Wait." Esther pulls away. She thinks of all the reasons Fanny would hate her switching places with Shira. One, she loves playing with Esther's hair and wouldn't want her to cut it. Two, she never lets her go anywhere. If Fanny found out, Esther wouldn't be allowed to ride a trolley until she was eighteen. Three, of all the places Fanny doesn't want Esther to go, the synagogue is at the top of the list. Fanny doesn't think God exists and tells Esther that even the best of God's lighting cues can't erase the suffering in the world. Fanny always says that if God is the director of the world, he's done a pretty awful job with world leadership—*bad casting all around*. Esther always thought her mother was wrong about the existence of God, but now she knows it for sure. "If there were no God, why would we have met right here, right now?"

"Exactly," Shira agrees.

The scissor blades seem to argue about how much hair they can handle, finally coming together with a *clip* and a handshake for a job well done. Shira plants a kiss on Esther's *keppie*, tells her, "The first cut is the hardest," and a lock of hair floats to the tile floor.

To calm Esther, Shira talks. "Papa is meeting with rabbis from nearby towns. He'll be home for dinner. Oh, you need to know about Rose. Rose Morgenstern is the best part of our visits to the hospital. She used to be the principal at Idylldale High School, but she's sick." Out of respect, Shira whispers *sick*. "Rose is the only one who sees how much I want to perform. She's the one who told me about the audition."

The more information Esther hears, the more relaxed she becomes. She focuses on the new life she's learning about and almost forgets how upset her mother would be if she knew Esther's long locks were trimmed. "Okay. Rose Morgenstern. Ex-principal. Possibly on our side."

"And then there's Miss Scheinfeld. She's helping with the food and party after the bat mitzvah. Papa has practically invited the whole town, but they don't know me as me. I'm just the Rabbi's Daughter." She stops and checks her work, pulling at sections of hair on either side of Esther's head, and their eyes meet. "You can make it through most social situations with a smile and a nod. A joke helps too."

"I don't know a lot of jokes." Esther's stomach lurches.

Shira laughs. "My father will appreciate that. Here's one, what do you call a crate of ducks?"

"I don't know."

"A box of quackers. Get it? Quackers, crackers?" Esther

laughs, but mostly at Shira, who is laughing at her own joke. Shira snips a bit more off the right. "Hey. What's my middle name going to be when I'm you?"

"Miriam. How about mine?"

"Ruth. Esther Miriam Rosenbaum, is it strange that we've never met before?"

"I don't think so, Shira Ruth Epstein," Esther says with a giggle. "How often do you come to the Heights?"

"Never. And your family has never been to the synagogue? Ever?"

Mayne kinder. You are smart. At this point in the story you have figured out that the people of Idylldale are Jewish, but what does that mean? There is a saying that if you assemble ten Jewish people in a room and ask them a question about Judaism, you'll get ten different answers. This is one of the most wonderful things about being Jewish: No one is Jewish in quite the same way.

But Esther doesn't know this yet. So when she hears Shira's question, she bristles.

To bristle is to have a tightening around your heart and prickling like hot needles on your skin. You might get cold but feel sweat in your armpits just the same.

For Esther, she bristles when she hears a voice that says: *You are not Jewish enough. You are not good enough.*

Shira has seen people bristle before. People bristle when there's too much or not enough Hebrew in a service—when there's too much or not enough God—when there's too much or not enough salt in a soup. Shira does not want her new friend to bristle. She says, "Do you know the Yiddish saying, *Got hot zikh bashafn a velt mit kleyne veltlekh*?"

Esther translates. "'God created for himself a world with many little worlds'?"

"Yes. Even in Jewish Idylldale there are people who pray just in their homes, or in theaters, or in synagogues, or in the woods, or they don't pray at all. Some people arrive for services every Friday night and Saturday morning, but they only come to synagogue to be seen, and some people, like you?"—Shira holds out a hand to her new friend—"have never been to synagogue but have deep faith." She squeezes tight. "My father always says they are all in one of the worlds that God has created."

Up until this moment, it has been as if Esther had lost her sense of smell at a great table. Even though the feast was in front of her, she couldn't enjoy it. Now, she nods. Her senses recovered, she wants to taste all that Shira's life has to offer. "I can't wait to be in your world."

"Soon enough, but it's your turn to tell me about yours. Who do I need to know?"

"Millie, costumes. Joshua, piano. Levi, lights and *shtarker*."

"Millie, costumes. Joshua, piano. Levi, lights and *shtarker*. And what's your role?"

Esther shrugs. "I'm Fanny's daughter. *The bookworm*."

Shira looks at her like she just ate a liverwurst and onion sandwich. "Great. That's *one* part of being you that I could do without."

It isn't long before Shira fluffs the ends of Esther's hair and nods.

Standing side by side in front of the bathroom mirror, the effect is fantastic.

"Holy casserole," Shira says.

Esther giggles. "I couldn't have said it better myself."

CHAPTER EIGHT

DIFFERENT WORLDS

BEFORE THEY TURN FROM the mirror, Esther gasps. "My mole. I'll have to cover it, and you'll have to add one. Mother has plenty of makeup on her dressing table."

"My makeup is in my closet. Oh, that reminds me. You need to make me a map."

"Of what?"

"Your world."

Shira cleans the scissors and disappears to give them back to the newsie. She returns with a grease pencil.

"Map time?"

"Precisely."

The pencil, waxy like a crayon, but erasable on the mirror, works perfectly. Esther draws, and draws, and draws. There's the Heights. The inside of the Heights. The way to their apartment. The inside of their apartment. The delis. "I guess that's it."

"That's a lot, Picasso." Shira examines the drawings.

"Do you have it in your head?" Esther looks at her sideways in the glass. "Will you be able to remember?"

"Absolutely," Shira says. "This is the map to every dream I ever had, remember?"

"If you don't, it's okay. Mother and I walk home from the theater together."

"Don't you worry about me, ol' Essie." Shira smiles a sideways smile and rubs away the floor plans and maps. On the blank mirror, she draws the way to her house from the synagogue. She draws the route to the grocery store and the hospital. She draws a map of their house.

"Two stories?" Esther says. "Holy casserole."

Shira laughs at her own words coming out of Esther's mouth. "It's a modest house."

"It's a *house*." Esther shakes her head. "I've always lived smushed between an old rooftop water tank and Mr. Silverman. This is going to be so odd."

"For me too." Shira wipes away the maps she drew and writes with the grease pencil on the mirror: SPECIFIC PLAN FOR FOOLING OUR PARENTS AND MAKING OUR DREAMS COME TRUE.

Esther raises her hand.

Shira rolls her eyes and calls on her. "Esther."

"Number one. Don't be too good. If you get the choreography on day one and sing like a nightingale, Mother will know right away you're not me."

"Good to know." Shira nods. "Number two, don't come back to your own world. Stay in your new space."

Esther points at her. "*Yes.* It would really mess things up if the two of us were in the same place at the same time. Oh, and three, don't tell anyone. Especially grown-ups."

"Absolutely. Mum's the word."

"Four. If you need something, go through Benny. Since he goes between the Heights and Scheinfeld's, he can help us."

Shira wags the pencil at Esther. "That's good. Should we have a meet-up spot?"

Esther shrugs. "The grocery store?"

Shira nods and says, "Parkway's," at the same time Esther says, "Siegel's."

"Hmmm," says Esther. "How 'bout right here at the station?"

"Friday noon? So I can teach you the Sabbath prayers?"

"Perfect. Mother never stays on schedule during lunch. She says take five and doesn't come back for fifteen. Speaking of which, we don't have a lot of time left before she's back from *her* hairdresser! You'll need to hurry to get these groceries." Esther takes the list out of her skirt. "Oh, you need my skirt too." Esther puts one leg in her new pants but misses the leg hole for the other side and hops around until Shira grabs her arm and steadies her.

"How do you wear this thing?" She twirls in Esther's skirt. "That's quite a breeze." Their giggles fill the bathroom and bounce off the tiled walls until their faces get serious with the weight of what's to come. "You ready?"

Esther thinks of how frustrating it is every time Fanny squashes her requests to study Torah. She grasps Shira's shoulders as if a knot she's been struggling with has finally untangled. "I'll put my body and soul into being the best bat mitzvah your father has ever seen."

Shira puts her hands on Esther's shoulders and looks into green eyes just like her own. Her heart might as well have wings like those fluttering pigeons cooing over there, cheering the girls on. "I'll put my body and soul into being the best talent show performer Nicky Sanders has ever seen."

The two girls hug.

"Okay. See you on Friday. Break a leg." Shira does a silly twirl, wiggles her *tuchus*, and walks toward the grocery store. She has Fanny's shopping list in her skirt pocket, the trolley directions to the Heights in her head, and the anticipation of a new mother in her heart.

Esther giggles at Shira's antics, the immensity of her new situation, and the silence that envelops her. She's about to get a father!

The air is charged with hope and longing.

ACT II

CHAPTER NINE

BENNY BELL, BELLHOP

OVER THE RIVER AND up the hill, Benny stands at attention on the entry stairs of Scheinfeld's Resort and Cottages. A more professional young man you never did see. He's the very picture of customer service in high-waisted black pants, a double-buttoned red jacket, and a red cap with gold braid accents. The thin black visor on the cap shades his dark eyes from the sun, yet his nose still sports new freckles from the almost complete summer season.

When a car pulls up, he jogs down the steps, which look like half a three-tiered cake, opens the car door, and gives the guest a hand. Despite his narrow shoulders, he lifts valises, directs children and their parents to the resort day camp, and runs errands.

Each time a trolley pulls up and pulls away, Benny is distracted from his duties. Will it deliver Esther or Shira? Or Esther *as* Shira? Of course, Miss Scheinfeld always seems to appear at his side whenever he's fidgety, and here she is.

Miss Scheinfeld has brown hair that falls in gentle waves around her ears and neck. She wears tailored jackets with a gold name tag on the left lapel, skirts that nip in at the knee, and sensible pumps that *click* on the marble floors and float on the carpeting. Now, she checks her most important accessory—her clipboard. "Benny. Don't dillydally. Mrs. Goldberg in 13 didn't get the Monday morning *New York Times*. In 22, the Goodman family wants extra towels. And the Meyer twins need tennis lessons."

Benny wishes she were less stern. But she has a whole hotel to run, so it is her job to be stern. Anyway, did anyone ever say to her father, who started the hotel, he should smile more? No, they did not. Now, when they say it to her, because she is a lady, she ignores them.

He pauses. What if the girls arrive while he's away from his post? But Miss Scheinfeld doesn't give him the luxury of his own decision.

"Benjamin. Don't just stand there, move."

Benny turns to run, but she stops him.

"No running!" Miss Scheinfeld calls. "Walk with urgency." She elongates the word *urgency* as if she is purring.

"Yes, Miss Scheinfeld." Benny brings his fingers to the visor of his cap in respect. After all, when she caught an eight-year-old Benny stealing pool boy tips, she didn't call the police or his mother or stepfather. She gave him a job. He folded napkins in the dining room, he organized swizzle sticks for the bartenders, he unloaded groceries for the chef until he could pay his debt. Then she kept him on as a junior bellhop.

Now, he stretches his senior bellhop legs and walks *with urgency* until he rounds the corner and accidentally kicks the wheel of an unsuspecting housekeeping cart. "Yowza!" he shouts, and jumps up and down holding his toe. A little boy walking by breaks into fits of laughter, so of course Benny crosses his eyes for greater effect. Even in pain he knows how to *work it into the act*. The boy's mother hands Benny a quarter, which he pockets with a thank-you as he grabs clean towels for the Goodman family in 22.

It's not until he's done with all these errands and at his front-entrance post again that he sees Esther . . . or is it Shira? She's wearing pants and striding in that confident way Shira has.

When she's close enough she shouts, "Hey, Ben, when are you off?"

Shoot, Benny thinks. *I guess Esther wouldn't agree to switch.*

But *kinder*, we know that Esther *did* switch, and now she has even fooled Benny! Maybe she has a career on the stage after all.

"She wouldn't do it, huh? Wouldn't switch places?" He shrugs. "You know, you can't blame Esther. She just is who she is. A little scared of grabbing life by the shoulders and shakin' it a little."

Esther narrows her eyes, gets close to Benny, grabs him by the shoulders, and shakes him a little. "You nincompoop! It's me. I fooled you." Esther steps back and bounces on her toes. "You really thought I was Shira?"

"Awww . . ." Benny nods reluctantly.

"Hey, and what's that supposed to mean—I don't grab life by the shoulders?" She slaps his shoulder to pass on her wound. "Come on. Want to explore the rabbi's house with me?"

He looks around, sure Miss Scheinfeld is waiting to pounce.

"Come on, Benny. Grab life by the shoulders." Esther bumps him.

"Okay, okay. I'm off in an hour. We'll take the trolley together."

"That's perfect—gives me time to go check out the synagogue."

"Look at you, breakin' rules."

"I'm a new person, Benny," she grins.

He points at her chest. "Hey, what's that?"

She looks down, and he chucks her chin.

"Phew! You're definitely still Esther. I'll meet you right here"—he coughs exaggerating—"Shira." Benny points her in the right direction and her heartbeat quickens as she follows the signs to the synagogue.

A long time ago, the Heights was like a glamorous lady in rich velvet and gleaming gold. These days she's more like a shabby but stately matron, with her fine clothes faded and jewelry in need of a good polish. But even when the Heights was new, her majesty paled in comparison to the luxury of Scheinfeld's. How could the Heights compete when Benny, along with a team of junior and senior bellhops, valets, housekeepers, maintenance people, and waiters, under Miss Scheinfeld's watchful eye, keep the resort polished and gleaming?

Esther can't believe her new life is rolling hills, tennis courts, pools, and cottages that surround the main resort. She can't help comparing it to the frayed carpets and peeling wallpaper that Shira will see. She looks out over the valley at the city of Idylldale. From here, the Heights is just another toy building in the valley below. The silver rope of river lassos the downtown on the Scheinfeld's side while train tracks fence the other. She takes a breath and sets off to find the synagogue trail.

She is amazed by the manicured green-and-pink landscaped paradise that has been so close, yet so far, all her life. When her mother was a teenager, she'd taught dance here, but then she got into the theater troupe at the Heights, became a star, had Esther, and neither she nor Esther ever came back. Now, Esther inhales the perfume of flowering hedges and, as she walks, chlorine and coconut oil. The sounds of people laughing and splashing fill her ears, and before she knows it, she comes upon a big, beautiful blue pool. "Wow," she says out loud.

In her neighborhood, kids splash in fire hydrants. Here, there are two diving boards! On one is a bathing beauty: a woman in a swim cap. Other women wait their turn to dive, while a man with a megaphone, the *tummler*, announces each contestant in the diving contest. The woman takes three steps, leaps, bounces, and does two whole spins before her dive slices the water. The children crowded around the diving well clap and cheer, and Esther can't help but join them.

Just then, the click of heels on the pool deck makes Esther turn. Even Esther, who has never met Miss Scheinfeld, recognizes her trim skirt, perfect hair, red lips, and clipboard. She freezes, hoping the woman will pass, but no luck. Miss Scheinfeld, concentrating on her clipboard says, "Please tell your father I say hello and tell him I'll deliver the Shabbos service participant numbers by Thursday. Oh. And we're checking on the brisket order for your party."

"Um . . . Thank you?"

Miss Scheinfeld looks up from the clipboard at Esther and tilts her head at an angle like a confused hen.

Be Shira! Esther tries again. "Thank you. I'll tell him."

"Fine."

How to get out of this conversation? "It's late. Gotta go. Holy casserole?" Esther ignores the inquisitive look on Miss Scheinfeld's face and hurries away up wide steps cut into the hill. Tiny white rocks carpet each stair and crunch under her feet, taking her up to a span of well-kept grass, and then . . .

"It's the synagogue," Esther breathes. It's as if she has to say it out loud to believe it. Three arched, heavy, honey-wooden doors framed in smooth pink stone are all that stands between Esther and her dreams.

Well, the doors, and having to trade places with another girl, and fool her father, and learn to be a bat mitzvah in a couple of weeks—but let's not get bogged down in the details. Oh look! She's taking the first step inside.

Esther stands in the synagogue's outer hallway on red carpet—a carpet quite a lot like the one in the Heights.

When the sanctuary doors close behind her, the silence is deafening. Goose bumps pimple her arms. As a small child, Esther used to wrap herself in the heavy velvet drapes that frame the stage at the Heights. The ark curtains, black with embroidered gold Hebrew letters, are more beautiful, more intimate, and more sacred. She feels taller somehow, and her head feels more open. Is she imagining this new expanse inside herself?

Esther extends her arms so both her right and left hands can tap the back of the dark wooden pews as she moves up the aisle. She wants to soak it all up through her fingertips— all the years that she never got to be here, the rhythms of the prayers, the song, the language, the community she never had. The prayer books smell like dried clay, and the carpet has a scent of mothballs mixed with baby powder. Shadow and light cast a Star of David in the aisle, and above her, she counts a circular Star-of-David window at each of the four directions in the dome above. She inhales it all.

At the very tippy-top center of the dome is a gilded star on a light blue field with tiny stars all around. Golden scrollwork bands the dome. There are so many similarities between the synagogue and the Heights—the ceiling, the curtains, the stage. For a moment, she wonders if her mother was right about the theater being a kind of worship.

Even though she knows the rabbi is away until dinner, she looks left and right before slowly mounting the *bima*. She stands under the eternal flame. She imagines the sanctuary filled up to the balcony as if it is opening night—no, not opening night, that's theater talk. She imagines that it is the High Holidays. She opens her mouth but nothing breaks the silence. Is it okay for her to pray here? Does she belong?

Before she can decide, the sanctuary door flies open, and there is a man—a giant man with brow and nose that might have been fashioned from a few lumps of clay a sculptor forgot to smooth. The giant man reminds her of the golem of Jewish folklore. He jumps at the sight of her, like an elephant scared by a mouse.

"Sorry, I didn't mean to scare you," she says, descending the stairs to the aisle. He has his hand on his heart.

"I didn't expect anyone," the giant says in a smooth, deep voice.

"I'm Shira Epstein. I'm the rabbi's daughter."

"You don't say. And I'm the Queen of Sheba." The Queen props the door with his work boot and turns to grab a toolbox, mop, and bucket. Ah. This is the handyman. She searches her memory, but she is certain that Shira never mentioned him. Good thing *Frank* is stitched in looping letters on his Scheinfeld's Resort and Cottages coveralls.

Esther runs up the aisle to hold the door for Frank with her back. "Ha!" she forces out, then manages a more realistic laugh. "Frank, the Queen of Sheba. It will be your new nickname. I'll tell the rabbi. The rabbi, who is my father. Who I'm going to see." She backs out the door, flustered. "Right now."

Phew, *kinder*. Frank knows Shira and it's certain that Esther should have known Frank. Running back to Benny, she feels as nervous as a junior bellhop. Shaking life by the shoulders isn't going to be easy.

CHAPTER TEN

A NEW STAGE

NEARING THE HEIGHTS, THE trolley slows, and Shira hops off before it even stops. Across the street, the theater marquee reads, in English and Yiddish, BEAUTY AND THE SHLE-MIEL STARRING RED HOT FANNY. Horns honk and cyclists ring their bells as she rushes across the busy street, but Shira is oblivious. She's imagining her own name in place of Fanny's. Would it say Shira Epstein? Would she have a stage name like Benny? Shirala is what Papa calls her. Lala Epstein? Maybe a different last name. Her mother's was easy to spell—Cooper. Lala Cooper!

A bicycle bell shocks Shira out of her reverie, and the telegram boy skids to a stop inches away. "I have a telegram from Alexander Malaise for Frances Rosenbaum," he says, breathless. "Are you Frances Rosenbaum?"

Her brain is swirling with the excitement of the moment when she says, "She's my mother. I can take it to her."

The boy pauses, but Shira extends her hand. "You look like you're in a hurry. Just hand it over."

He does, kicking off and zipping away to his next delivery. She shoves it into the pocket of Esther's skirt, turning her attention to the brass doors once again.

Entering the theater, she imagines her future and feels the warmth of the bright awning lights even in the daytime.

There's a *thump* and a leg appears stretched across the big brass doorway. "Snap out of it."

"Huh?"

"You'd think you don't even know your own name." A short, stocky fireplug of a man lowers his leg and closes his newspaper. "I said, 'Why ain't you usin' the stage door, Esther?' And you don't even answer."

"Oh," Shira says. The man rubs at the stubble on his wide jaw with a hand the size of a prayer book. Shira realizes this must be Levi—lighting and *shtarker*—the one who won't laugh at Benny's jokes. "*Levi*. Can't a girl do something different once in a while?"

"Well, sure," Levi stammers. Esther usually demurs and hustles off to read. Such a bookworm, that Esther. She rarely challenges him. "Sure," he says with a gruff mutter. "Different's okay."

"Anyway. I'm working out a new bit for the *Nicky Sanders Show* and want to see the stage from the audience's point of view."

"You really gonna do it? The show I mean?" Levi asks. "Me and Joshua, we've been making bets."

"Of course I'm doing it." Shira nods and inches past his chair. "I'll be great, I'll win, and I'll get the prize money."

"Well, well. All worked up," he says with a guffaw. "Just like Fanny."

"Yup! Just like my, um, mother." Shira strolls into the theater as if she's been there every day of her life, but once she's inside, being Esther can wait a few more moments. First, Shira wants to be herself—salt and all.

She puts down the grocery bag, extends both arms, and runs her fingertips over the back of each red velvet chair as she passes. She basks in the clouds, moon, stars, and planets painted on the ceiling above. She runs down the aisle, pounds up the side stairs, and rushes to center stage.

"Oh, what a beautiful morning!" she sings. The song is one that her papa likes from a musical about people on farms. She swirls Esther's skirt as she prances and wiggles in front of the curtain. She twirls back again and tells the joke about the tailor and the bad suit that she told to Rose Morgenstern. Laughter from the side of the stage freezes her the same way Esther froze when she ran into Miss Scheinfeld.

"This is what you do when the cat is away?" Fanny is feline in the graceful way she leans against the theater's brocade wallpaper. She rests her chin on her white-gloved fingers as if they were paws, and her eyes seem to see every part of Shira.

"Fanny. I was just . . ."

"*Nu?* You're too old to call me *Mother* all of a sudden? Give me a hug."

Shira blushes. "Mother. I'm sorry. I guess I was in character?" She makes her way down the stairs and up the aisle into Fanny's embrace.

Gardenias and the scent of the salon cling to Fanny's soft shoulders—so different from the smell of old parchment that wafts around her papa. Shira gives a little extra squeeze. Fanny will only be her mother for the next two weeks, so she knows she shouldn't get attached.

Fanny holds her at arm's length. "In the character of whom? What happened to your neck?"

Shira claps a hand over her neck. "It's just makeup. My mole is still there . . . of course."

"And what's this?" Fanny tugs her hair gently and frowns. "You cut it without asking me?"

Of course, *mayne kinder*, Shira has had her hair at her shoulders the entire time you've known her, but compared to Esther's the last time Fanny saw her, it's short.

"I cut it without asking," Shira repeats, searching her mind for a way out. "Mama, I've been thinking about the audition."

Fanny pushes out her lips and nods. "I'm so glad you're embracing this, *bubbele*. When you win the talent show, we'll be on TV. Well, *you'll* be on TV, but if I play my cards right . . ." Fanny's voice softens then, as if she just remembered something. "I have to talk with Levi about the lighting during act 2."

It's impossible not to watch Fanny. Her heels are silent on the red carpet, and there's an elegant *swish* from her green skirt. She looks every bit the celebrity. On her way to Levi, Fanny turns back to Shira. "I know you're dying to pull a book out, *bubbele*, but please . . . let's decide on a song?"

Shira nods. As soon as Fanny leaves through the big brass doors, Shira sighs. Phew! Being someone else is exhausting! Certainly Fanny would have said something by now if she thought Shira was an imposter, right?

First things first—take care of Esther's star-shaped mole. Or Shira's lack of one.

Through curtains and down a metal stairway to a hallway lined with pipes, Shira seeks Fanny's dressing room. She looks up and down the hall and slips inside a room with a star on the door. In front of her, there's a mirror bordered with round lights. Shira flips a switch on the edge of the table and blinks in the brightness. Catching her own grin in the mirror, she jumps up and down in a small circle. "I'm here, I'm here, I'm finally here!"

The mirrored vanity, covered with makeup, looks just like the ones in the movie magazines she hides from her father. To her right, there is a rod full of costumes with all kinds of theatrical shoes underneath. To the left of the door, there are cards from admirers on a corkboard with a few dried flowers pinned beside them.

There are tags on each hanger that she examines, sliding them over the metal rod: *Beauty and the Shlemiel Act 1*, *Beauty and the Shlemiel Act 2*, and so on. For the final scene, there's a ball gown. Even though the costumes are sized for Fanny, Shira tries on the gown and twirls, making the big skirt float around her.

She sits at Fanny's lighted mirror, pulls her hair up on her head, and is transported. "Dahlink!" she says as if she were Russian royalty. "So nice of you to have come to opening night. You vant me to introduce you to Nicky? Oh, right this way."

The lights, the costume, the stage, Fanny—it's all dazzling, and she never wants to leave. Eventually, though, she hangs the ball gown back on the rod, dresses in Esther's clothes, and settles to create the mole on her neck. The hinged wooden box on Fanny's table is magical and contains everything you'd need to become someone else. Shira sorts through a long blond braid hairpiece, a tin of nose putty, and a burnt cork for making an actor look sooty or bearded.

Finally, she finds a light brown tin of pancake makeup. She dabs it on her neck in the shape of a tiny star with a damp round brush, layers and blends it with her skin, then uses a puff to powder and set the makeup.

Voila! "Esther Miriam Rosenbaum," she says to her reflection, "welcome to your new world."

CHAPTER ELEVEN

THE RABBI'S HOUSE

BACK IN THE WORLD of Scheinfeld's Resort and Cottages, Esther and Benny have boarded the trolley to Shira's house, and Esther is telling him about the huge handyman.

"Frank called himself the Queen of Sheba?" Benny laughs. "He works at Scheinfeld's too. Good plumber. Nothing to worry about." But Esther worries anyway. It is her usual way of being. Disembarking from the trolley, they are far enough from Scheinfeld's that the noises of the resort and cabins have faded.

Esther is used to a world filled with calls from the knife grinder, directors yelling "action," ambulances, trolley bells,

general ruckus, and flashing lights. She is used to Levi drawing the line when the Bellows twins, Larry and Aaron, shout
at the night performers from their seats in the front of the
theater. She's used to selling tickets to boisterous families at
the matinee. All the noise has made her quieter and more
observant.

But Shira's world has none of this chaos. As she walks,
Esther relaxes. She notices birdsong and a child's distant
laughter. Even the houses are quiet: Every one they pass is a
two-story shingled home, surrounded by a picket fence, with
a front door centered between two windows. Evenly spaced
trees shade each yard and a side door leads to a driveway.

On the opposite sidewalk, a mother pulls two children in
a red Radio Flyer wagon. The children wave, and Esther and
Benny wave back.

"I always wanted one of those," Benny says with melan-
choly in his voice.

"What do you think people do here? I mean to live like
this."

"I don't know." Benny shrugs. "But I'm sure they don't
work at the textile mill like Ma."

"Maybe they're the mill bosses," Esther says. "Here. This is it."

They stand under a large maple tree whose leaves flutter in the light warm breeze. Esther knows Benny was right when he said she rarely *shakes life by the shoulders*, yet here she is—about to go into a strange house and live with a stranger.

Let's remember, of course, strangers are a regular part of Esther's life. Performers come; they rehearse; they produce a show at the Heights; they celebrate at the apartment; they leave on the next train. Some stay a little longer than others.

But no matter how many strangers you meet, it is odd, to say the least, to walk into someone else's home.

"Come in with me?"

"Let's see what a rabbi's house looks like," Benny says.

Benny is through the side door and two steps into the rabbi's kitchen before Esther whispers as if she is in the Idylldale Public Library. "Ben. Take your shoes off. It's so clean!"

Shira's kitchen isn't palatial, but the kitchen in the apartment Esther shares with her mama—nothing but a hot plate and refrigerator—is inferior in every way.

They both slip off their shoes and leave them on a welcome mat with the image of a blue windmill. One step later, Benny stubs his toe on a miniature iron windmill just inside the doorway. He hops around the kitchen, and Esther can't help but laugh. "Yowza," Benny says. They were both holding their breath before, but now the laughter releases their nervous energy. Benny wiggles his body like a *loksh*. He's more noodle than boy, this Benny!

In the living room, Benny looks like Goldilocks, sitting first on one chair and then on the next. "Look at this cabinet TV!" He admires the red wooden doors and the gold speakers.

He turns the TV volume knob, and with a *pop*, a star of light appears in the middle of the screen that warms up and expands into a clear black-and-white picture.

The volume fills the room and, guilty, Esther says, "Turn it off, turn it off."

"What, why?"

Esther can't think of a good answer. She doesn't know why, not exactly—just that Benny has barged into the rabbi's home as if it's his own, while Esther is trying it out as if she's testing a tender ankle. Each step forward makes her wince a little, but she knows it's good for her to build this muscle.

"What if Shira isn't allowed to watch during the day? What if the rabbi comes home and feels that it's hot and I get in trouble? Fanny does that." Fanny's tiny portable TV has an antenna made from a wire hanger. The two of them often nudge each other out of their shared bed to wiggle the hanger back and forth when the picture gets too fuzzy.

"You sound *meshuge*. You know that, right? Come on." Benny thunders up the stairs and Esther follows on cat feet. At the top she finds two bedrooms and a bath in between.

"What'll it be like sharing a bathroom with the rabbi!" Benny muses.

"I'll manage," Esther figures, shrugging. "This is way fancier than sharing with Joshua's sons and stinky Mr. Silverman."

"They sure do like windmills," Benny says, pointing at the ceramic cup and soap dish.

Esther shrugs. "Maybe someone in their family is Dutch?"

In the rabbi's room, suits hang together in the closet, then white shirts, then blue ones, then ties. He has two pairs of black leather shoes, two pairs of canvas sneakers, and what Esther imagines are two pairs of brown leather shoes, because there is a distinct empty space where one pair is missing its second set. "He's neat as a pin," she says with admiration, but Benny has already moved to the door across the hall. "Wait, Ben. I should see my room first."

He opens the door and swishes his hand. "After you, Miss Rosenbaum."

In Shira's room, Esther feels more comfortable. "*Miss Epstein* from now on, bellhop," she says. She admires Shira's white spool bed, a white bedside table and dresser with yellow drawer fronts, and a standing full-length mirror. The walls are white too, but who could tell? Posters torn from movie magazines and signed photos of performers and comedians are everywhere. The one from Nicky Sanders says, *Thanks for watching the* Nicky Sanders Show. *To my biggest fan!*

"Hey, he already knows her! She's a shoo-in for his show." Benny looks unusually starstruck.

But Esther just cringes. "Do you know how many of these I've signed for Fanny?"

Benny looks surprised. "You mean when I'm a big star, I get to pay someone to sign my name?"

"Or have a kid with good handwriting. Anyway, I don't know that I'd call Mother a big star." Esther tours the room slowly, stopping to touch the silver brush and comb set on the dresser. She picks up an invitation from a small stack. "Rabbi Samuel Epstein requests your presence as his daughter, Shira Ruth, is called to the Torah. Saturday, August twenty-first." She nudges Benny. "Our birthday."

"Right. But that's less than two weeks away!"

"I know. I've got a lot to do," she says. She and Benny plop onto the bed, tucked tidily with a yellow chenille spread. "How am I going to learn all I need to learn in two weeks?"

"*Less* than two weeks. But if anyone can do it, you can, Ess. You're the best studier I know."

"Thanks, Ben." Esther spies the clock on Shira's bedside. "Oh no. Benny, you've got to go." She pushes him off the bed, and they hustle down the narrow stairs back through the living room and into the kitchen. "And *I* have to make dinner. What am I gonna make? Do they have canned soup? Where's a deli when you need one?"

Benny puts a hand on her shoulder and points to the refrigerator. "It's okay, Esther. Looks like you're making baked chicken and boiled potatoes tonight. At least the directions are included in the name of the dish."

On the refrigerator, Shira has posted, with a windmill-shaped magnet, the dinner menu for the month of August. Each date has the groceries needed and a note that says "Shira" or "Papa," and some have a cryptic number in the corner. Esther isn't sure what this number is, but she's grateful that Shira is organized. For tonight Benny is right. It says "Baked Chicken & Boiled Potatoes/Shira," with a little number "218" next to it.

"I've never baked a chicken or boiled a potato." She's starting to sweat. "Which do I do first, Ben?"

Ben shudders and steps back. "Don't ask me. My neighbor Mrs. Sapoznik cooks and watches baby Avram when Mama has a night shift at the mill."

She drops her face into her hands, then remembers what Benny told her when he thought she was Shira. *Take life by the shoulders and shake it a little.* She plants her feet with forced confidence and puts her hands on her hips. "You better go, Benny. If I start now, I'll be done by the time he comes home."

Benny puts on his shoes and stands half in and half out of the doorway. "You can do it, Ess." And with that, the kitchen door clicks shut behind him.

Kinder, even for the most practiced chef, it takes some time to get used to a new kitchen, and Esther is not a practiced chef. Living downtown, she and Fanny are close to my deli and the bakery and just a trolley ride away from the kosher Dragon Emporium. Why cook?

Yet that doesn't make Esther feel any better. She squeezes her eyes against a sudden burn of tears and shakes them away. "You're Shira. You can do this," she says. She puts her head in the refrigerator, emerges with a whole chicken, and transfers it to the sink.

Opening cupboard after cupboard, she finds pans. There are pans on a shelf labeled DAIRY and others labeled MEAT, so at least Esther doesn't have to worry about the food being *treyf*. She pulls out a flat pan from the MEAT shelf. *That'll give it plenty of room to cook from all sides*, she thinks. On her search through the cupboards, she comes across a basket of small, round red potatoes and another basket of onions. Thank goodness.

Now, she opens the oven.

Mayne kinder, when you want an oven to get hot, what do you do? You spin a dial to the right temperature, or push some buttons, and on it goes. Shira's oven has a small gas source that a person has to ignite with a match. Esther once overheard Fanny and some of their performer friends tell a story about Mr. Such-and-such whose oven had too much gas and the match created a fireball that singed off his eyebrows.

Esther is terrified that this will happen to her, but if she's going to bake this chicken, she'll need to light the oven. On the wall beside the stove there is a ceramic long-handled-match holder (painted with blue Dutch windmills, of course). "I have to remember to ask Shira about these windmills," she says to no one, but her own chatter steadies her a bit.

"Okay," she continues as she opens the oven door. "I just have to light the match and stick it . . ." She spots the hole in the metal bottom of the oven and takes a deep breath. "In there. Light the match first or turn on the gas first?"

She strikes the match and, with a shaky hand, gets it poised in the hole. She turns the oven knob. With a *whir* and a *whoosh*, a blue flame burns beneath the metal bottom of the stove. Esther exhales. Ladies and gentlemen, *she's done it!* Eyebrows intact!

She sets the oven to 450 degrees, which to Esther seems just hot enough to bake a chicken. She plunks the chicken on the flat pan, thrusts it into the oven on the middle rack, and closes the oven door. *Ta da!* she thinks. *Chicken, baking.*

She uses another match to light the stove burner and sets the potatoes to boil in a large pot of water on a high flame. Now, she figures, she has a bit of time. "I'm not so bad at this," she says, patting her sweaty forehead and neck. "Oh no. The mole. I need to find her makeup."

In Shira's room, Esther opens the closet and pauses. It doesn't feel polite to rummage through someone else's things. "She's definitely looking through my stuff too," Esther tells herself, and drops to her knees to dig through movie magazines, sneakers, and black Mary Janes before she finds three shoeboxes. Opening the first, she discovers envelopes wrapped in a red ribbon. Okay, they're not makeup, but they *are* interesting.

She unties the ribbon and takes a card from its envelope with a postmark the year of their first birthday.

Dear Baby Shira,
Happy Birthday!
Wishing you and your father health and happiness.
Love, Uncle Coop

The cards for their second, third, fourth birthday are all essentially the same. Whoever Uncle Coop is, he doesn't seem to have much in the way of imagination. She gives up on the fifth card, reties the ribbon, and sets that shoebox aside.

In the second shoebox is Shira's favorite birthday present, the too-small tap shoes. She opens the final box, and under a movie magazine she finds—makeup! In Shira's mirror, she dabs cream on her neck that matches her skin color, and her mole vanishes.

Backing out of the closet, Esther hears a sizzling, sloshing sound that makes her heart run and feet follow down the small staircase, through the living room around the corner and . . . *oy vey!* The pot of water is boiling over, and *shmaltz*-smelling smoke fills the room.

"Oh no."

She waves her hands back and forth to cut through the smoke, turns off all the gas, and opens the oven door. More smoke! "Fresh air," Esther instructs herself, and props the kitchen door with the iron windmill.

As the air clears, she sees a white, foamy mess pouring over the pot and crusting on the once clean stove top. Below, the *shmaltz* has liquefied, dripping over the edge of the flat pan, burning on the hot oven floor, and leaving a black mess.

"Stupid!" Esther shouts. But really, how could Esther have known this would happen? She drops to her knees. How, she wonders, does someone clean burnt grease out of an oven?

"Shirala? Why is the door open?"

Yes, *mayne kinder*. When dear Esther is on her knees with her head in the oven, sweat pouring down her face, and oven mitts on her hands, *that's* when Rabbi Epstein, her understudy father, comes home.

"Shira! What's happened here?"

"Rabbi? Rabbi! I'm so sorry. I used the wrong pan. Not the dairy pan, but this flat one, and the chicken fat dripped all over and burnt. I'm sorry. I already said that, but I am. Sorry. I've ruined your dinner. Please don't be angry."

After all this time of wanting to meet the rabbi, Esther doesn't want to encounter the hawk-eye look that Shira said was so scary, but she does look, and he's not at all scary. He is a tall man, youngish and trim, with brown hair and a noble nose. His bushy eyebrows knit above cinnamon-colored concerned eyes. "Angry? Hush, Shirala." Before Esther knows what is happening, the rabbi kneels with her, his hands on her cheeks. Esther is sure that he'll see the truth in her eyes, but all he says is, "I don't care about the dinner, Shira. Are you hurt? Are you okay?"

"I'm fine, Rabbi."

"'Rabbi'? Why do you keep saying that? Shira, are you ill?"

Sweat stings her eyes and tears trickle over her cheeks. She thought she could do this, but she can't. She can't lie to a holy man. Even though she desperately wants to learn Torah from him, even though she wants Shira's friendship, even though number three of the Specific Plan for Fooling Our Parents and Making Our Dreams Come True states *mum's the word*, she has to confess. "I'm not your daughter.

I'm a performer's child who wants to be a bat mitzvah, maybe even a cantor someday, and so I'm here in Shira's place. Shira is fine. She's at the theater."

The rabbi's brown eyes change from concern, to anger, to something that looks like he might be in on her joke. "Wait." He shakes a finger at her. "This is one of your pranks?"

"N-no, Rabbi."

He places the back of his hand on her forehead. "Oh my, Shira. You're so hot! Are you right in the head? I'm your papa."

Esther shakes her head vigorously. "No, Father. Papa. I mean yes, Rabbi. I just . . . The heat of the oven, and I'm a little dizzy. That was the wrong pan, I guess." She's so scrambled she might as well be eggs. She really does feel sick now.

"I'll call the doctor. Let's get you to bed."

"No, Papa—er, Rabbi," Esther protests as he scoops her legs, carries her upstairs, and deposits her in Shira's bed under the yellow bedspread.

"Hush now. I'll get you a cool cloth."

Esther hears the water run, the cloth wrung, and carpeted footsteps approaching. The rabbi sits, patting and cooling her head. He smells like books, and Ivory soap, and coffee. Esther told him the truth, or tried anyway, and well, she figures, there is no point worrying him further. "I can call you Papa?" she asks.

"Shh," he quiets her, but she doesn't have anything more to say. As he kisses her *keppie*, she has one thought.

Shira is the luckiest girl in the world.

CHAPTER TWELVE

THE DELI

SHIRA CLEANS UP THE dressing-room vanity, careful to return everything to its place, and turns off the bright lights around Fanny's mirror. Her eyes drift to Esther's bookshelf on the wall, with its single prayer book. "Nope. Sorry, Papa. I won't pray here. Not even once." Just then, her stomach growls. "But I do have to eat." She already picked up groceries on her way to the Heights: oil, tuna, cheese, tomatoes, crackers, and canned soup. She could make something out of that, but it seems more like lunch than dinner.

Baked chicken and boiled potatoes are on her dinner menu at home. Hopefully, she thinks, Papa and Esther have already eaten. She closes her eyes and tries to picture the map to the apartment that Esther drew on the mirror. She told Esther she would "absolutely" remember, but the images are fading and fuzzy now.

From the wings, Shira is entranced by Fanny bathed in a blue spotlight on a dark stage. The light changes to red, then green as she sings, "*A bisl zun, a bisl regn, a ruik ort dem kop tsu leygn* . . ." It's one thing to be hungry for food, but Fanny's Yiddish song, playful, upbeat, and silky smooth, fills a hunger Shira didn't know she had.

"That was beautiful, Mama," Shira says when Fanny stops singing.

Fanny turns briefly, "Thank you, Essie. Levi, which color looked best?" Shira remembers her hunger all at once. How long do these rehearsals last?

"Wait, Mama. When can we eat?"

"It's taking longer than I expected to nail this."

"Few more minutes," Levi yells from the lighting booth high above.

"I'll start dinner," offers Shira. "What's on tonight's menu?"

Fanny tears her attention from the script she holds to stare at Shira. "Menu?" She calls up to Levi, "Essie wants to know what's on the dinner menu."

Levi calls back, "Isn't tonight beef bur-gon-yon?"

Fanny lifts her right pinkie and affects a French accent. "Oh, François. Bring me your best wine to go with my boeuf. And a warm loaf of bread, s'il vous plaît."

"Ah. Oui, oui!" Shira teases back. Her father never plays like this. Still, she isn't any closer to dinner. "But if there's no beef at Chez Rosenbaum . . . what *is* for dinner?"

"Dinner is what it always is." Fanny presses two fingers to the top of her nose and speaks more gently. "I'll be done soon, darling. I'll meet you at Morty's."

A deli sandwich for dinner. What could be better?

Under the awning at the Heights, Shira tries to get her bearings in the dark. Everything looks different with neon flashing in the storefronts. Inside that *keppie* of hers, Esther's map drawings from the trolley station mirror are a smudgy swirl of grease pencil. She's sure that Esther drew the apartment behind the theater, and a little less sure about the location of a deli or two. Hopefully, she can find Morty's. An ambulance screams around the corner, and she jumps away from the curb; a trolley bell clangs, sending her back another step with her hand on her chest to slow her hopping heart. "Holy casserole." She didn't realize the trolleys ran so late into the night. "Quiet down now," she says to the ruckus.

She pushes away an annoying desire for the quiet of her own block with its little houses that look the same. She misses the regularity of her refrigerator menu and their cheerful blue windmills.

With belly grumbling, Shira walks through pools of lamplight toward a flashing neon DELI sign, but across the street is *another* sign that says DELI. Shira is a performer and a comedian and often tells the joke about the Jewish man stranded on a desert island. He builds two synagogues—the one he goes to and the one he doesn't go to. Here it is in real life. Two delis—the one Fanny and Esther go to and the one they don't go to. Which one is right?

Ah, *kinder*. It's very hard to make decisions on an empty stomach. I always say, eat first, think later.

Here's how she figures it out. She goes to the door of the first deli, opens it, and calls in. "Hey! Is Morty here?"

"What, are you crazy?" a voice barks back. "You want to buy day-old meat, go across the street. You want the best sandwich around, stay here."

"I'll keep that in mind!" Shira says, and goes across the street. Day-old meat or not, Morty's is where Fanny has her line of credit.

A sign on the door says BEST KNISHES IN IDYLLDALE. What? It's not bragging if it's the truth—and if there's one thing you want from a deli man, it's the truth.

Shira enters and bells tinkle above her. "Morty?" she calls again.

This is where I come into the story. Now, as a narrator, there are certain privileges. I could describe myself as a strapping young Morty who lifts crates of potatoes like they are feathers, goes to the theater every night, and has a full head of hair. But, *mayne kinder*, that wouldn't be the truth.

The Morty in this story, the real deli man, is old enough that whatever hair used to be on the top of his head seems to have migrated under his nose, leaving a ring of cottony white hair over his ears. Neither his round glasses nor his mustache hides his gentle eyes and smile. He welcomes Shira in and wipes his hands on his white apron. "Come, come. The regular?"

She's not sure what Esther's regular is, but Shira takes a chance and nods. Her stomach growls again.

"Ah. Let's feed the beastie inside, yes?" He hands her a knish. "No charge. I didn't sell all of them. Can you imagine? And they're no good the day after."

Shira accepts the golden dumpling and bites.

Kinder. You already know that when you are very, very hungry, almost anything—with the exception of liverwurst with onions—tastes good. But Morty's knish is not just anything. Did I already say they are the best in Idylldale?

What? You never had a knish? Imagine the lightest, fluffiest mashed potatoes wrapped in a piecrust and baked to perfection. You got it? Yes? No. It's not like that at all. A knish is better than a fluffy biscuit, better than a melt-in-your-mouth donut; a knish is love. And just between you and me, I didn't have extra knishes. They sell out, every day. But I always put one aside in case Esther comes by. What can I say? Even a deli man has his favorites.

Shira bites through the golden-brown crust into the oniony, salty, soft potato. Her eyes close. Her face lifts as if to God. A delighted sound escapes. Shira is in knish heaven. "These are amazing."

"And don't let Saul tell you any different." He juts his chin toward the other deli across the street.

"Will you teach me to make them someday?"

"If there's one person I'd share Bubbe's secret recipe with, it'd be you." He cups her chin. "But who could cook in that apartment?" Now he nods across the street and to the left.

Phew. That's how to get home.

Morty comes out from behind the counter and presents a sandwich to Shira. She peeks under the bread and blanket of lettuce. Esther's usual is a dry salami on rye with lettuce? With eyebrows raised, Shira asks cautiously, "May I have some mustard please?"

"You want I should add mustard?" He pushes out his lips in surprise. "You always tell me you'll never ever in all your life eat mustard."

Shira shrugs. She can't believe Esther doesn't like mustard. How is she going to get out of this one? "Well, Levi tricked me into tasting his with mustard the other day and . . ." She shrugs. "What can I say, I liked it."

Morty nods. "Ah. One time, my mother . . . you mustn't tell anyone . . ."

Shira shakes her head and crosses her heart.

"Okay. So one time my mother's *bubbe* came to visit and there was no money for lamb chops. And what did my grandmother do?"

Shira shrugs.

"She served pork chops. And you know what?"

"No." Shira is wide-eyed and aghast. Pork chops aren't kosher. "What happened?"

"Bubbe never knew the difference. And God knew they were poor. Here. Salami and lettuce on rye . . ." Morty pauses for effect. "With mustard."

"Thank you, Morty."

Shira inhales the sandwich. She knows now that Saul across the street is full of baloney because the salami is fresh as can be.

"Hey, Morty. Have you got my kid in there?" Fanny calls through the tinkle of doorbells.

"Another late night, eh?"

"Don't have a choice!" She gives him a kiss and leaves lipstick lips on his forehead. "Thanks for feeding her. Good night, you beautiful old man." Is Morty *blushing*?

Well, that's one way to take his mind off Esther's newfound love of mustard.

Outside, Fanny beelines for an apartment building across the street, and Shira rushes to keep up. The building looks just as Esther promised, skinny and long, with four floors and fire escape decks that obscure the windows. It also looks like every other apartment building on the block—all of them leaning on each other shoulder to shoulder. Good thing she didn't have to find it on her own.

At the roof level, a stone cap is topped by an iron banister. From up there, how far she could see? Certainly, she'd see the lights of the Heights a couple of blocks away. Could she see the train tracks behind the building? The river on the way to the synagogue, and her own home where Esther is probably fast asleep by now?

Inside, they climb the switchback stairs all the way to the top floor without Fanny saying a word. By floor three and a half, Shira is gasping and grasping the thick wood railing hand over hand.

"Too much reading. Not enough dancing," Fanny says, looking down from the fourth floor.

"Maybe you're right," Shira says, catching her breath, then pinches her nose. "It stinks!"

"I guess Mr. Silverman used the pot already."

Shira has never shared a toilet with other families, but right there, at the top of the stairs, is an open door that leads to a lone toilet.

"Let's go, *bubbele*. Time for bed." Fanny unlocks the apartment door, pushes a wall button, and light spills into the hallway.

A grateful Shira hurries across the black-and-white checkerboard linoleum to get away from the stink.

In the apartment, she gazes out the two windows that lead to the fire escape. She's never had one, but she's heard New York City congregants tell of nights spent on fire escapes to get relief from summer heat. Do Esther and Fanny do that too?

"Hey, head in the clouds." Fanny closes the slatted blinds with a *snap*. "Go on. Off to the toilet," Fanny says.

Oh dear, *mayne kinder*. Esther and Fanny have choreographed their whole going-to-bed routine. Will Shira be able to keep up? No, she won't.

After the bathroom, and unsure of where she's supposed to wash up, Shira blocks the door. "Esther, please, out of the way." Fanny takes her by the shoulders and repositions her by the kitchen sink. "Wash your hands and put on your nightclothes."

Mayne kinder. Do you remember how tentative Esther was exploring Shira's home? She even needed Benny to help. Here, Shira must hunt alone for her own pajamas! In the far corner, behind a flowered silk folding screen, a hanging rod heavy with clothes is rigged from the short wall to the long wall.

No pajamas.

An electric lamp, a travel trunk, a bedside table made of a DAIRY crate with two books from the Idylldale Public Library—all these things, Shira finds. But no pajamas.

She is pulling open one dresser drawer after another when she hears the doorknob turn.

"Still dressed!" Fanny cries in mock horror.

"I can't find my nightclothes," Shira says, and the whine in the poor girl's voice reveals how exhausted and mixed-up she is.

Fanny reaches for the same drawer as Shira, and they bump heads hard. "Ow!" Fanny squints her eyes. "Essie, are you all right? You're acting *meshuge!*"

Rubbing the growing knot on her head, Shira tears up. She swallows hard and Fanny's face softens. "Oh, *bubbele*, it's okay. I'm sorry. Here. Let me help you." Fanny tugs on Shira's shirt to help her undress, but Shira steps away.

"I'm okay," Shira says hurriedly. She finds some privacy behind the screen and wiggles into Esther's nightgown. Away from Fanny's scrutinizing gaze, Shira wipes at her eyes, takes a few deep breaths, and tries to relax again. "Mama, I came up with some ideas for my audition song."

"Ah. That explains why you're acting so odd."

"Yes. That's *exactly* why I'm acting odd." Shira's response is quick and decisive. She crawls into bed and switches on the bedside lamp.

In the dim room, Fanny changes behind the screen. "So tell me, darling. What songs can I say no to today?" She uncaps the Noxzema, and Shira is overwhelmed with the scent of menthol and eucalyptus. It reminds her of the VapoRub her father rubs on her back when she has a bad cough, and all of a sudden, she can't quite catch her breath. Her heart hurts a little with missing him.

"Yoo-hoo. Esther. What's the song?"

"Um . . ." At least daydreaming is something that she and Esther have in common. "'Mairzy Doats'?"

"Ahhh," Fanny sighs. "It's a classic, but trust me, they'll hear that a million times at the audition."

Shira's trying not to get hypnotized by Fanny's motions—the way she pins her hair into a twist, the way she moves her mouth to make her cheeks taut, the way she applies the thick white cream without hesitation. She's never lived with a mom or even had a girl come to her house for a sleepover. "Next idea?" Fanny finishes wiping and rinses her face in the sink.

"'Boogie Woogie Bugle Boy'?"

"Too old for you." Fanny climbs into the bed.

Without the makeup and the put-together clothes, Fanny isn't the star of the Yiddish theater troupe at the Heights. She's just a regular woman—Esther's mother.

And for now, she is *Shira's* mother.

Fanny snuggles into bed, sings a lullaby, and strokes Shira's hair. When Fanny leans in for a kiss, Shira wants to pull away, but she doesn't want to be found out. She misses her own father's kiss, yet she longs for a mother. She leans in.

Fanny's lips on Shira's forehead are warm and loving. "We'll talk more about it tomorrow, *bubbele*." She turns to face the windows and curls away from Shira. "The light, Esther. It's late. No reading."

Shira is relieved to follow this direction. With a *click*, the apartment is dark. Only the streetlamps cast slices of light on the pink walls and the oval, braided rag rug.

Suddenly, the excitement of sleeping away from home for the first time threatens to come out in a rush of giggles. She clamps her lips tight. Rose was right: Doing the wrong thing could bring joy.

CHAPTER THIRTEEN

TORAH PORTION

IF YOU'VE EVER GONE on a journey to a relative's house or to a hotel, perhaps you've woken up a little confused and unsure of where you are. Most likely though, you do know *who* you are. Poor Esther. She opens her eyes to the sunlit poster of Nicky Sanders and has to remind herself that she has become Shira Epstein, the Rabbi's Daughter.

Esther fixes the smudged makeup covering the mole on her neck and heads downstairs where the rabbi is squeezing grapefruits for juice.

"Good morning, Papa," she tries. In Yiddish, "father" is *tate* or *foter*, but the rabbi made it clear in the middle of her kitchen fiasco that Shira called him *Papa*. She's surprised how natural the word sounds when she says it. For a moment, she feels a twinge in her heart. Where is her own father?

Rabbi Epstein's brows rise and his shoulders shudder, and he laughs. "Oh, my Shirala. You sure had me going last night. A performer's daughter who wants to be a cantor?" He wraps her in his arms and lifts her off the floor. "I won't always understand you. But I will always love you. You're feeling better this morning?" He releases Esther and her feet touch the floor again. "Here. Sit. Your favorite will make everything all right."

"Thank you so much, Papa," she says. Esther has never had grapefruit juice before. She pines for her usual morning drink. As Rabbi Epstein pours coffee for himself, she imagines both her hands wrapped around a steamy mug of her own, with two scoops of sugar, chatting with Morty at the deli.

"Shirala, I need to go to the hospital today, but with you being sick, I don't think you should come. Can you practice your Torah portion on your own today?"

Esther gulps the grapefruit juice and makes a sour face. Shira likes this stuff? She scrapes her tongue against her teeth. "My portion?"

When you are born, there are a lot of things you don't get to choose. You don't choose your mother and father, what they do, or how much money they make. You don't choose the holidays they celebrate, what they believe, or the history of their ancestors. Some of these things you grow to embrace, and other things not so much.

Fanny made sure Esther knew the importance of Yiddish theater and culture to the Jewish community, but never took her to synagogue. Still, Esther spent plenty of time in the library learning more about her religion. She learned that the Torah was divided into books and then into bits that worshippers in synagogues from Idylldale to New York City and beyond studied week by week. This bit is called a portion. And oh, dear. Esther never asked Shira the specific Torah portion she'd been assigned for her bat mitzvah.

"First you forget that I'm your papa, now you forget your own bat mitzvah?"

"No, no. August twenty-first! And my Torah portion is . . ." She eats a too-large spoonful of cereal, hoping he'll fill in the blanks.

"Deuteronomy 5:16. Honor thy father and mother. It's all in your folder in my study." The rabbi watches Esther chew. "Shira, you know that's not polite. Talking with your mouth full."

Esther swallows. "Sorry, Papa."

He holds up a finger, which Shira would tell you is a sign he's going to say something he thinks is important. "Once you're a bat mitzvah, you're no longer a child in the eyes of the congregation. You must be more responsible, Shira. So you can study on your own today. If you're sure you don't need a doctor?"

"Father, I'm fit as a fiddle."

"Well, if you are fit as a fiddle . . ." He pokes Esther's tummy, surprising her into a giggle. "I'll be off to check on Mr. Aaronson." He ties his shoes.

But Esther has been waiting all this time to study with the rabbi, ask him questions, and have meaningful conversations about infinite solutions. "Are you sure I can't study *with* you?"

The rabbi, a crease between his brow and his hand on the doorknob, pauses. "*With* me?"

"Yes. I thought I could do it myself. I"—she takes a leap here—"told you that I could do it myself, but I'm having problems. Especially with my pronunciation. And the melodies. I just . . ." She pauses. This might not be what Shira would do, but Esther has to ask. If not, she might never know what it's like to study with this learned man. As if she is taking a bite of double-decker sandwich she says, "I need your help."

Rabbi Epstein considers her. "But you always say you like studying alone."

"You always say that the hardest thing to do is to ask for help, so I'm asking. And . . . I want more time with you. It's just . . . you've been at the hospital so much lately," says Esther, hoping against hope that it's true. "Stay. Stay and teach me." Her plea hangs over them like branches on a *sukkah* roof.

"My Shirala." He strokes her cheek. "How can I refuse this request? I'm as happy as a man with a new suit. I'll see Mr. Aaronson in the afternoon instead."

And so, the two of them don jackets and head for the trolley. Esther grins. Shira and Benny's harebrained scheme is working, and her whole body is filled with the same excitement and nervousness that comes with an opening night.

Here's something that you should know, *kinder*. Yiddish and Hebrew, sort of like Esther and Shira, may look similar, but they are not exactly the same. Esther speaks and reads

English, and she reads and understands Yiddish. But the vowels for Hebrew and Yiddish are a bit different, and they have different origins. And Esther doesn't know the melodies to *leyn*, or chant, Shira's Hebrew lines from the Torah for the bat mitzvah.

While their Specific Plan for Fooling Our Parents made clear that neither of the girls could be too good at their new task, now Esther is petrified about being too bad. Won't the rabbi know she's not Shira the second he hears her try to chant? On the trolley approaching the synagogue, Esther clutches and twists her shirt and doesn't say a word to the rabbi, who asks her three more times if she's feeling well. Why didn't she think through this idea before she blurted it out? She wishes Benny were here to calm her nerves, but there's nothing he could do now to help except to tell her to shake life by the shoulders. Arriving at the synagogue, Esther lets go of her shirt, shakes out her hands, and follows the rabbi into the beautiful building, trying to stride like Shira and her father.

This time, though, Rabbi Epstein has a bounce in his step! You see, *Shira*, the real Shira, prefers to be in her room, listening to records, choreographing dances, and making herself up into new characters. She doesn't want to study *with* him. Rabbi Epstein's dreams of being beside Shira on the *bima* are coming true. Finally, he thinks, his daughter is taking to his life's calling!

Mayne kinder. Do you remember that Esther has a small bookshelf in Fanny's dressing room and library books by her bed? Esther loves books, and hoo boy, has Rabbi Epstein got books in his synagogue office. Books with leather spines and gold trim. Books with deckle-edged pages and dusty and enticing book smells. Each book uncovers a world! As the rabbi turns on lights and rifles through his desk, Esther runs a finger over the books in the case, removes from the shelf *A Woman's Commentary of the Torah*, plops right onto the floor, and starts reading.

"Shira?"

Esther reads.

"Shira," he says a little louder, and this time she realizes. She is Shira!

She tears herself away from the book and stands. "Sorry, Papa." She lifts the book of women's commentary. "Some of these women are rabbis. Did you know a woman can be a rabbi?"

His jaw releases and his eyebrows relax, and he pulls her into an embrace. "Who are you?" the rabbi says into her hair.

What a thing to ask her! "Holy casserole," Esther says with Shira's force. She wiggles out of his hug, sure that their closeness will reveal her lies. "I'm the rabbi's daughter with awful Hebrew pronunciation and maybe piano lessons in my future?" She's taking a risk with this performance, guessing with details gleaned from her time with Shira. She's had years onstage, and even if she doesn't like it, of course she can act!

Rabbi Epstein sighs, convinced, for now, of her Shiraness.

"Well, so I'm trying to do better. These women can be my inspiration, don't you think?"

He hands her a stapled booklet and keeps one for himself. "Let's practice your *parsha*."

"Right. My Torah portion. Of course." As with all Hebrew and Yiddish books, it opens and reads from right to left. Esther looks at the title. Because she knows Yiddish, she can sound out the consonants, but where are the vowels? It's like sight-reading a musical score without some of the notes! "That's a great place to start, Papa. Reading the Hebrew, but you know what? I love singing. What if instead of me *reading* the Hebrew, you *leyn*, and I repeat small phrases? It'll be just like we're on the *bima* together."

The rabbi's face brightens, his eyebrows unfurl, and his eyes smile. Esther is encouraged. She continues, "Then you can tell me where my pronunciation is off, and we can practice over and over, like we're rehearsing for a show."

Oops. That makes the rabbi frown. "This is not a show. This is a religious ceremony. At the end, you will be seen as an adult in the community." He hardens his eyes and looks down his nose at her. "Shira Ruth Epstein, I need you to take this seriously."

A middle name is never a good sign. "Of course, Papa." She tucks away the book and feels her heart tap-dancing in her chest. "I'm ready." Finally, finally, she is studying the Torah!

They start with the *aliyah*, the prayer before reading the Torah, *Bar'chu et Adonai ham'vo-rach!*, and Esther recognizes the beginning as if the words have been in her heart all her life. Back and forth, Rabbi Epstein chants a line of prayer or text, and Esther follows as best she can. Sometimes she gets transported by his baritone and the prayer. She watches his finger on the study booklet and tries to see what he sees, filing it away in her photographic memory. Ah, the vowels are the dots and dashes under the letters. When the Hebrew words start coming together, it tastes better than a hot-out-of-the-oven knish.

"Pause, Shirala." Rabbi Epstein's face is loving but scrunched. "Your pronunciation is better today, but I thought you knew these lines better by now?"

"Well," she coughs. "I'm trying to see it with fresh eyes. A fresh start. To really take it seriously."

He sighs. "All right. Let's start again. At the beginning."

"Take it from the top!" she says with a huge smile. And this time—he smiles with her.

CHAPTER FOURTEEN

THE COSTUME MISTRESS

ALL AROUND IDYLLDALE, IN the early morning, the store-fronts yawn and stretch. The bookseller wheels his cart of books onto the sidewalks, the fruitseller pyramids a rainbow of berries and citrus, and the knife grinder calls out in his singsong voice for new business. When the neon signs are still dark, after the fresh knishes are cooling and the soups are simmering on the stove, the deli takes a deep breath and readies for the day. In this quiet time, Shira bursts in, door-bells dancing.

"I couldn't sleep," she declares.

"I didn't expect to see you until after ten." Morty hands Shira a knish and she takes a huge bite.

"Mmm. So good, Morty."

Morty beams.

"I dreamed that I couldn't breathe because a mason mortared my nose shut. When I woke up, Fanny's—I mean Mama's—elbow was in my nostril!"

Shira takes the mug Morty's holding out. Coffee. Her father drinks the bitter, black liquid every morning. Now, Morty's eyes are on her as she blows and sips. Shira makes the same face that you make over stinky Brussels sprouts—nose and eyes scrunched, tongue stretched to her chin. She is afraid that she's given herself away until she opens her eyes and Morty is offering a bowl with a spoon. "You forgot the sugar," he says.

"I forgot the sugar, all right!" Shira laughs. "You know, Morty. I think I'll take this with me. I'd like some time in the theater before Mama gets there."

Morty nods with a knowing grin. Knowing *what* though? Shira doesn't know. He can't have guessed that Shira is Shira and not Esther—it's too unbelievable! "Thanks, Morty," she tells him. She snags the cup and an extra knish and heads straight to the alley behind the Heights. *Dump* goes the coffee into the dirt. What she wouldn't do for a nice cool glass of grapefruit juice.

Inside the theater's stage door, she feels along the wall for a light switch, turns them all on, and makes her way to Fanny's dressing room. She touches up the mole-colored makeup and considers the *siddur* on Esther's top shelf.

If Shira were at home, her father would have already reminded her to study for her bat mitzvah. But now she is at a new home. A home that puts a prayer book on a hard-to-get-to shelf, a home where a trip to the hospital means you're sick—not visiting. A home where she's free—no, she's *encouraged*—to be as funny as she wants to be. *You're the most dramatic Rabbi's Daughter I've ever met*, Esther had said. "Yes. I am," she says to the mirror, and sticks her tongue out at herself.

On the stage, she imagines the theater seats full of people, with a spotlight on herself in a sparkling gown like the one she saw on the *Nicky Sanders Show*. She twirls and one-two-three waltzes around the stage in a large circle. She hears the voice of her long-ago dance instructor from Scheinfeld's, the Captain, saying, "Posture!" and "Eyes up!" and "On your toes." At center stage she catches her breath to belt, "*There's no business like show business.*"

Mayne kinder, it's never good to keep emotions inside. They twist your *kishkes*, your intestines, and make you feel heavy. Right now, all of Shira's sadness and desire are switching places with delight and joy. She is onstage and about to audition for a television show! The joy bubbles like a fresh, cool spring. She can't hold it inside. "Ta-da!" she says to the empty seats, standing with her arms over her head. She does a somersault, and another. Then, with arms out to the sides, she spins and spins until she is dizzy and falls flat on her back, laughing some more. Shira takes deep breaths until the theater stops spinning. "*Button up your overcoat,*" she sings softly. "*When the wind is free, take good care of yourself, you belong to me.*"

"Is that what you've chosen?"

Shira startles to sitting. There stands a stout woman in a blue snapped smock with a yellow tape measure around her neck and brown-and-gray hair mushrooming above her soft features. "Um . . . Good morning, Millie." There's no one else it could be.

"Good morning to you too. Your mother left me a note that you might be onstage, but, ack. She didn't mention that you cut your hair! How'd she handle that?" Not stopping for a response she says, "Is 'Button Up Your Overcoat' for the audition? I wasn't sure if you'd do it at all."

"Fanny—Mama—put her foot down about the audition, so I didn't have a choice. I'm trying to embrace it." Shira feigns disappointment. "And I haven't checked with her about the song. She's still asleep."

"No time for sleeping. Let's go." The woman moves quickly in spite of her short legs and extra weight. She looks back at a stunned Shira. "Follow."

Shira jumps to her feet and has to steady herself from the rush of blood to her head. "Mama hasn't approved the song choice yet," she warns.

"There's a lot of humor possibilities with 'Button Up Your Overcoat.'" The woman counts on her fingers. "Ruin your tum-tum, flannel underwear . . . Costumes could be funny too. The overcoat could go on and off, there could be layers."

As they descend a staircase that takes them under the stage, Shira marvels at large props from past shows. There's a park bench, a sofa, and a stop sign. The stage crew have hung ladders on hooks on the walls, and shelves of drippy-sided paint cans stand in rainbow order. Finally, Millie opens the door to the costume shop.

Shira gasps. Rods and rods of well-organized clothing, shelves of different kinds of shoes, sandals, and boots in all sizes, wigs on head-shaped stands, hats on hooks, gloves in baskets, sewing machines, and cutting tables with rainbows of fabric. "It's beautiful!"

"What is?"

Oops again. "Um." This place would not be new to Esther. "I just . . ." Her eyes dart around and land on a couture creation coming together on a dress dummy. "That dress, it's beautiful."

"That old thing? It's getting closer, in any case. I did try it with a chiffon. Much lighter than the brocade. Let's look through the overcoats."

"Maybe a set of rain boots?"

"Perfect!" She produces a yellow trench coat and red rain boots. Shira slides on the coat no problem.

"Millie? Have you got Essie down there?"

"I'm here, Mama!" Shira says, loving the taste of each syllable.

Fanny inserts herself into the shop as Shira sits and unties her saddle shoes to put on the boots. "Oh, the chiffon is much better than the brocade, Millie."

Shira and Millie share a knowing look. "Your daughter thinks so too. Here. Right foot. We're working on costumes for the showcase. Imagine 'Button Up Your Overcoat' with layered costume changes, losing layers of clothes as you go, until . . . you know where that ends!"

"Now *that* might work," says Fanny. "Not like Helen Kane though. No boop-boop-a-doop."

"No, no. It would be more innocent. More . . . Esther!" Millie pinches Shira's cheek. "Right foot, I said."

Shira slips her socked foot into the boot as far as she can. "It's too small."

"Whad'ya mean it's too small? It's a size six."

Shira's eyes widen. "Um . . . Maybe my feet grew?"

Fanny stops and covers her mouth. "Is our little girl becoming a woman?"

"Uh oh. What else is growing?" Millie says, and waggles her eyebrows up and down.

They both laugh and Shira covers her whole face. *Oy,* the drama of this place. Thank goodness it was Rose Morgenstern and *not* her father who told her about getting her period. "Please, Millie. Ma. It's just my feet."

Millie puts the bottom of the rain boot against the bottom of her foot. "Okay, okay. Seven. Let me see what I've got."

While Millie digs, Fanny floats to Shira's side. Absently, she finger-combs Shira's hair, and Shira loves it. "Let me hear a few bars, Esther."

"Of 'Button Up Your Overcoat'?"

"Mm-hm." She twists a section of hair.

"Wear your flannel underwear, when you climb a tree, take good care of yourself, you belong to me."

"That sounded great, *bubbele*. Millie, what if she takes off the layers and ends up in the long johns? That'd get a laugh."

Millie sits back on her heels and purses her lips at Fanny. "What a great idea," she says. "Too bad I didn't think of it." Shira realizes that this is not the first time Fanny has presented one of Millie's ideas as her own.

"Then let's do it," says Fanny. "*Nicky Sanders Show*, here we come."

CHAPTER FIFTEEN

HONOR AND OBEY

IN A LITTLE OVER a week, Esther will be on the *bima* next to the rabbi chanting her bit of the Torah, her portion, and explaining its meaning. Now that she has committed her few Hebrew sentences to memory, she chants her portion when she brushes her teeth in the morning, and it starts her day with joy. She chants her portion when the trolley is late, and she is more patient. She chants when she gets into bed at night, and it puts her to sleep. Her Torah portion has become a comfy chair she settles into, a cozy blanket that smells like home.

Rabbi Epstein is pleasantly surprised. Who knew that all he needed to get Shira to take her bat mitzvah seriously was put his foot down? Perhaps, he thought, he had been spoiling Shira before.

(We know, *kinder*, that all he needed was an entirely different child.)

Esther is over the moon that she is learning so much. And learning makes you ask questions, don't you think? So Esther must be learning, because she has plenty of questions. For one thing, her portion of the Torah is all about honoring and obeying your parents—two things she's *not* doing, but she needs to deliver a speech on this topic at the bat mitzvah.

Rabbi Epstein sits at his desk, which is littered with bits of leftover crust and wax paper sandwich wrappers, proud that his daughter is engaging with the text.

Esther, deep in the throes of learning, paces back and forth, balling up her own sandwich wrapper and an empty bag of Nibbles potato chips, tossing them in the trash can without even realizing she's doing it. "Surely, there are some moments where honoring one's parents is at odds with obeying your own desires? What are we supposed to do then?"

"Well, Shirala," the rabbi says. "Parents are older. They have more life experience and can see the longer view when it comes to making decisions. Don't you agree?" He wipes his mouth with a napkin and taps the English translation of the Torah on his desk. "Your mother and father are the reason you exist in this world, anyway. So, a child should not contradict or oppose his or her parents in a dispute."

"If the child never contradicted or opposed the parent, there would be no dispute."

"That's clever." The rabbi smiles, and Esther basks in it.

"I mean, shouldn't children think for themselves? Isn't that one of the ways we honor our parents? And if we do, won't that sometimes contradict with the desires of our parents?"

All that pacing. She might wear a path in the carpet, don't you think?

"Not according to civil or religious law. Adults, parents, play that role. Parents always have their child's best interests at heart."

Esther stops her pacing and plants her hands on the rabbi's desk. "In a perfect world, maybe. But what if they don't? What if parents just put their own lives and dreams ahead of their children's?" Wasn't this what Fanny did all the time? Or was it that she put the needs of the theater ahead of the needs of her own daughter?

And who was her father? Some person named Mel? It was true, she would concede, that his presence was critical in her existence, but did he have Esther's best interests at heart when he *left* her? She ponders this aloud, "Or what if God takes the parent away so that they never have an influence on their child at all?"

"Shira Ruth." Before, Rabbi Epstein looked like their debate was making him happy, but now he moves his hand to his heart as if he's been stabbed. "God made sure that you had all of your mother's goodness before she died. Her life essence and love."

In a moment, Esther remembers Shira saying exactly this, with tears in her eyes. Sharing candy in the Trolley Transfer Station seems so long ago that Esther can't believe it has been only four days. Four days that have brought Esther and Rabbi Epstein closer together and allowed her to ask questions and learn the things she always dreamed of knowing. She was so caught up in their discussion that she had forgotten she was supposed to be Shira—and now Esther is afraid that she has wounded the rabbi. Feeling that she has disobeyed in just the way the Torah warns against, her words race. "Not Mama, Father. I'm not talking about Mother. I'm speaking . . . what's that word you said, when something is possible but not real? *Hyper*-something?"

"*Hypothetically?*"

"Yes. *Hypothetically*. About . . . a girl I see at the grocery."

"Oh." Shira's father takes a deep breath. "You know, Shira. Your mother would be so proud of you. Especially of the difficult questions you're asking. Come. Sit with me a moment."

Esther leaves her well-worn path in the rug to hug him even as he sits. He pats her hands and reaches out to the photo on his desk. As he traces the frame with his index finger, the formality he wears like a heavy overcoat slips from his shoulders. "When your grandparents died, your mother had to raise her brother." He points at one of the two men crowded around a woman with a brand-new baby. "Your Uncle Coop." Esther looks closer. Shira's Uncle Coop has kind, familiar eyes. Shira's mother's hair is mussed, face flushed—she cradles tiny baby Shira in her arms on the very same night that Esther was born down the hall. In the picture, Rabbi Epstein looks so young and full of light.

Esther holds out her hand to take the picture, but Rabbi Epstein intercepts.

"Remember. It's the only one."

Esther pulls her hand back from the cherished photo, and he gently lays the frame, photo down, on the desk. Still, it pulls at her like the stray dog to the deli alleyway. She can't help thinking that Uncle Coop looks familiar. Don't people write information on the back of photos? There are a few simple clips keeping the black velvet backing in place— keeping her from knowing more.

"Now," Rabbi Epstein says. He sits up straighter, intertwines his fingers, and remakes himself into the rabbi. "Tell me about your friend from the grocery." When he clears his throat, Esther refocuses.

"Right, well, her father left before she was born, and her mother always put her own success ahead of my . . . *friend's* Torah education." It's what Esther's always believed, always known, but voicing it in this way, against her own mother, sounds harsh out loud. She adds quickly, "In all other ways she's a wonderful mother. She is loving and generous. She just . . . wants her child to be successful, I suppose." Esther realizes this too is true.

"I don't presume to know this family, Shirala. But if the mother is keeping your friend from Torah, she might be threatened by her daughter's faith. Maybe they can try studying Torah together?"

It takes all of Esther's patience not to roll her eyes at this suggestion. Fanny would never agree to that. "And if she doesn't have time?"

"Well then, your friend might study on her own or seek out other teachers. The only time when a child should question their parent is when the parent keeps them from studying the Torah."

Esther gets sly. "So in that case, it's okay to disobey?"

"Then, the child is obeying God," Rabbi Epstein proclaims, pointing to the heavens.

"Oh! I know!" Esther almost feels she is thinking of this idea for the first time. "I could teach her. I could meet her on Friday when you are working on your *d'var Torah*, your speech for Shabbat service."

"That would be wonderful!" The rabbi claps his hands. "A *mitzvah*."

A good deed! But is it all good? Esther would get to learn from Shira, yes, but the rabbi has put his stamp of approval on the deceit going on under his very nose.

"Shira," the rabbi continues gently. "I want you to know . . . you and I? We'll have many disputes in our life. Even when we disagree, it doesn't mean we stop loving one another."

Esther lifts a finger with an uneven cuticle to her mouth and gnaws at it. He loves Shira, but she is not Shira. In changing places with Shira, is Esther obeying God or disobeying Fanny? How could she and Shira do this? She worries her nail until Rabbi Epstein gently lowers her hand to her lap.

But *kinder*, should Esther feel so guilty? I mean, does the bread feel guilty when the baker doesn't give it the yeast it needs to grow? No. It is the baker who must nurture the dough so it will rise. And any baker worth their salt can see the difference between a bagel and a bialy! What does it say about how well these parents know their daughters that they can't tell one from another?

CHAPTER SIXTEEN

BANISH THE MUSE

SHIRA, ONSTAGE WITH FANNY, tingles with anticipation. From her slim black pants that skim her ankle to her clean white top, her dance rehearsal clothes feel magical.

"We've only got three days left until the audition," Fanny says impatiently. "Are you ready, darling?"

"I guess," she says, trying to cork her enthusiasm the way she imagines Esther might.

"Then let's dance." Fanny blocks out some steps as if she's been doing this all her life. Because she has. She looks back at an eager Shira and says, "*Bubbele.* I'll teach it to you slower. One set of eight at a time."

Esther's words ring in Shira's head: *Number one. Don't be too good.* "I think I've got it," Shira says, and intentionally makes two mistakes. Fanny corrects her.

By midmorning, they've gone over the blocking and choreography for most of the dance. Shira has made both fake and real mistakes. Fanny, pleased that Shira is picking up the steps, has added an umbrella. "Ooo. Do I get a hat too?" She taps a bit, using the umbrella as a cane.

"Pay attention," Fanny says, clapping out each syllable. "Here we go . . . Stomp, kick at the imaginary puddle of water, swing the umbrella up and over your shoulder, and on the last note lunge forward and open the umbrella over you."

Shira tries the move.

"Over your right shoulder."

She tries again.

"Good. But I want the lunge forward to be bigger. We should think that you're about to fall."

And again.

"The umbrella opens *over* you. If it's in front, we can't see you."

Finally, Shira does the move perfectly—and adds on her own count of eight and a ta-da at the end.

"Darling, please follow the choreography, I've crafted it just so."

Now *this* Fanny sounds just like her father, a perfectionist about every Hebrew syllable for her bat mitzvah. She rolls her eyes and Fanny sees.

"Esther." Fanny's voice is strained and hard. "Time is short. Auditions for children are difficult and live television is serious. You've got to be spectacular."

"Okay, okay."

"It's not okay!" Fanny's words come out like a runaway trolley car. "You are nose-in-a-book for half your life, while I try to give you everything I never had, and you are always only trying to get away from the theater as fast as you can, and now you have a sudden burst of creativity? Essie, I am not one to banish the muse, but just this once—stick to the plan! If you do . . . who knows what this audition could bring us? Bring you, I meant. You!" She throws her hands in the air. "Take five, then rehearse some more with Joshua."

Watching Fanny march down the stairs to the costume closet, Shira is stunned. She thought she was doing so well. Better than Esther would do for sure. She wants to get on

Nicky Sanders's show—of course—but why does it matter so much to Fanny?

From the balcony in the Heights, Shira's chocolate-colored curls and the music pages are all we can see. She faces Joshua, the accompanist, over the upright piano. To Shira, the notes look like an army of ants running across the pages. Who would have taught her to read music? "Your boys sure do get up early," she says, stalling.

"The walls are as thin as paper," he says. "I'm sorry about that. Minna and I try to keep them quiet but . . ."

"Let's go," Fanny interrupts as she descends into the orchestra section and takes her seat. "From the top."

Joshua nods. A flop of dirty blond bangs falls to cover his round spectacles over a check mark of a nose. He rakes his bangs to reveal his blue eyes and long lashes, a movement he makes many times a day. "Okay," he says. "I'll play the two-bar intro and you come in."

Shira squints her eyes, hoping that magically the notes will arrange themselves into something she can decipher, but they do not. Thank goodness she knows the tune, and she can read the words fine. *Figure it out.* She exhales, taps the pages together into a neat pile, and nods back.

"Ready and . . ." The notes of "Button Up Your Overcoat" float to the balcony and Shira sways her head with the rhythm, but—

"Right there, Esther. You missed it," Fanny calls from row A (*Ambition! Awards!* and *Alone!* Fanny refuses to sit anywhere else) of the red velvet orchestra seats without looking up from her newspaper. *Show Business,* the industry weekly newspaper with all the TV and theater auditions from New York, Chicago, and Hollywood, is open to the page titled OTHER NOTABLE AUDITIONS where the Nicky Sanders audition is listed.

Shira rounds the piano to stand behind Joshua. The wrinkle above her nose is deeply creased. "Sorry. Right. Two bars. Which is . . ."

"It's in four-four," Joshua says to Shira's blank stare. He circles the note on the score with a pencil and taps it with the eraser. "Eight beats in."

"Right, four-four. I know when." No. She didn't. All of Shira's singing know-how comes from listening and memorizing, not reading sheet music. "I meant, could you play my first note? That one?" She points to the note in the circle.

"Every Good Boy Does Fine," he sings in a scale. "Does, Does, D." Joshua plays the note three times in quick succession. He furrows his brow. "It's D above C in the treble clef."

"Why didn't you say so!" Shira can tell she's pushing believability, so she turns on the charm. "The walls *are* paper thin. I'm just tired."

Joshua shrugs. "I'll count you." He plays and says, "A five, six, seven, eight." He nods a big nod, and Shira sings.

When she sings *"eat an apple every day,"* she pretends to juggle apples. She rubs her stomach and gives a sad face when she sings *"you'll get a pain and ruin your tum-tum."*

Joshua smiles at all the right times. "Very good," he says. "Fanny? What do you think?"

"Either they'll love her or hate her, but they'll know in the first minute." She flicks the paper, and a *snap* echoes through the theater. "Did I ever tell you about the audition when I didn't even open my mouth? Hardly got two feet in the audition room and the director shouted, *'Next!'*"

Even if Esther has heard this story before, Shira is hearing it for the first time. Are auditions so cutthroat? Even for children? Now she *really* has a pain in her tum-tum.

Thankfully, as Joshua works Shira throughout the morning, she loosens up. He's impressed that her range has increased even though she's trying not to be too good too quickly.

Shira had no idea there was so much to singing. Joshua teaches her to open her throat and lift her palate to get the best sound. He teaches her to feel the vibrations in her nose, to feel the difference between her head voice and chest voice. He tells her about vowels and ending consonants and how they can make her enunciation clearer.

Let's face it, Shira is in heaven. "I wish I'd learned this earlier."

"I didn't think you cared."

"I do now," she tells Joshua.

Fanny puts down her paper and stares at Shira on the stage. She sounds assured, supported, stronger than she ever has. All this time Esther has been so timid, so focused on studying Hebrew. This is a kid who loves learning but was too smart for school; of course she'd want another teacher. Fanny feels a twinge of guilt for losing her temper, and now her competitiveness kicks in. Listen to this kid sing! Her daughter might actually win this thing. It could be life changing for all of them—little do the girls know exactly *how* life changing.

"Maybe we could put in some jokes?" Shira says. "Knock, knock— "

"Less is more," Fanny counsels as the stage door slams open and Shira jumps.

"Levi needs to fix those hinges," Benny calls, emerging from behind the curtains. He wiggles a deli box in the air. "Lunchtime, everyone!"

"It's not even noon," Fanny says.

But Shira presses her hands together. "I was up early, Mama. It's lunchtime for my stomach." She knows she has to meet Esther at noon and hopes that Fanny will give them a break and lose track of time like Esther said she would.

"Oh fine. Take ten."

Benny hands Shira a parcel in waxed paper stained yellow from the inside.

Fanny raises one eyebrow as her daughter unwraps the sandwich and takes a humongous bite. Fanny gave her the same eyebrow raise when, after the shoe size incident, Millie took all of Shira's measurements and came up with a slightly larger bust measurement as well. "So mustard is no longer *uck*? I guess everything changes when you become a woman," she stage-whispers to Joshua. A stage whisper is like a regular whisper except your voice is loud enough for the whole theater to hear you.

"Mama!" Shira says, slapping her head in embarrassment. Still, she's grateful for the motherly way Fanny notices her.

They eat. The sounds of their chewing and *mmm*-ing and *yum*-ing fill the theater.

"What's this?" Benny says, and points to a place on her chest, but Shira doesn't fall for his trick like Esther always does. She slaps his hand away.

Fanny watches this and thumbs her hand at Shira. "She's wise to you, Benjamin."

Shira and Benny freeze like hunted mice.

"All right, I gotta go make some calls. You two take a break. We'll run through the dance again later."

Watching Fanny swoop away, like a beautiful hawk you can't take your eyes off of, Shira asks, "Does she know?"

"What would she know? That we've replaced her daughter?"

"Right. That'd be ridiculous."

"Preposterous." Benny crosses his eyes and sticks out his tongue, and the two of them let out their fear in uncontrollable laughter.

CHAPTER SEVENTEEN

MEETING AT THE TROLLEY TRANSFER STATION

ESTHER PACES AT THE Trolley Transfer Station. Maybe her mother did one of her eat-in rehearsals when no one gets a break and you grab bites of a sandwich between scenes, and Shira will never get out. What then?

The trolleys arrive, their bells clanging. They switch tracks with a rumble and leave again. She checks the clock on the top of the station and looks down the block again. Finally, Shira and Benny jog up. Shira's smile is as clear as a polished deli display case, and she throws her arms around Esther. "Sorry. I was working on my tap technique. I don't have the shoes yet, but Mama says . . ."

Esther pulls away from their hug. "*Mama?*"

"I mean Fanny. Sorry. *Fanny* says if the audition goes well, we can get some."

Ben shakes his head, and Esther shakes away her concern. After all, she's been calling Rabbi Epstein *Papa*. "So? It's going well?"

"So good." Shira does a few dance steps. "I'm just practicing the number over and over. You?"

"It's everything I imagined—except maybe harder! And you all have so many books! Your father said it was a *mitzvah* for me to teach you—my 'friend from the grocery store.'" She tugs at the bottom of her shirt. "What he doesn't know is, *you'll* be teaching *me*. I didn't know I'd have to say prayers for the candles, wine, *and* bread in front of the whole congregation! I need your help."

A summertime Shabbat service certainly isn't as well attended as one after the High Holidays in the fall, and it won't be as well attended as next week's bat mitzvah celebration, but after almost a week studying and living with the rabbi, today she'll stand next to him as his daughter in a very public way.

"And this morning you started the dough for the knishes? And the challah?"

Esther bites her lip. "Um . . . No."

"Didn't you read the recipe?"

Esther stares blankly.

"On the menu. The page number was right there."

Benny and Esther turn to each other. "Ohhhh," they say, nodding. Esther continues, "I had no idea what that number was."

"Yeah, me neither," Benny agrees.

"Oh boy." Shira doesn't mince words. "Esther, do you have your allowance money with you?" When Esther nods, Shira says, "Give it to Benny. Ben, go to the bakery and pick up a challah. At Morty's, get as many knishes as they have."

Ben salutes Shira. "If Miss Scheinfeld ever needs a replacement, you're a shoo-in," he says, and jogs away.

The two girls find a bench and sit silently for a moment. "I'm so sorry, I didn't realize about the cookbook . . ." says the girl who hates making mistakes. (Ah, someday she'll learn that mistakes lead to learning even more than perfection does.)

"Water under the bridge," says the girl who would rather move forward than dwell in the past. (But the past informs the present, does it not?) "Let's start with the candles. You said that in the past you've used birthday candles in place of Shabbat candles?"

"That's what we had around the house," Esther says. A few days ago, this fact would have embarrassed her, but now she is proud that she did what she could to celebrate the Sabbath. "I know I cover my eyes and draw in the warmth with my hands three times."

"Yup. You close your eyes after you light the candles, so any joy from the candles comes after the blessing. Do you know how it starts?"

Esther nods. The beginning of the blessing is the same as the one she learned for reading Torah. She says the Hebrew words (*Barukh atah Adonai Eloheinu melekh ha'olam . . .*), and Shira stops to teach her the endings for each of the three other prayers. Their voices harmonize with the squeal of trolley brakes and conductor announcements. A few people stop and listen.

Together, Shira thinks, *this isn't so bad.*

Together, Esther thinks, *this is wonderful!*

Benny, carrying a bag from Morty's, arrives as they finish up. "Knishes and challah, as ordered."

Just then a trolley stops, depositing its passengers, and off steps the deli man. All three children freeze as if this might render them invisible, but too late.

Mayne kinder, this is the moment everything became as clear to me as well-strained chicken broth in a good matzo ball soup.

Morty points at each of the girls in turn. "Aha!" he says. "I knew something was fishy. After all, it's very rare that someone suddenly decides to like mustard."

You can imagine the awkwardness of this situation. Luckily, in very awkward situations, Shira has been taught to fall back on manners. "Shira Epstein," she declares, extending her hand. It feels so good to hear her own name coming out of her own mouth! "Pleased to make your acquaintance."

"Hoo-ha? *Epstein* as in *Rabbi Epstein?*"

"Yes," Shira's voice rises with surprise. "But how do you know him? I haven't seen you at temple, Morty."

Morty waves the comment away with a swish of his hand. "A man my age has lived many lives." As if to illustrate the fact, the packages he carries start to slip. The girls take his parcels and Benny helps him to the bench, so they are four across.

Esther bites her thumbnail.

Shira bounces her leg.

Benny worries the bag from the deli.

Morty strokes his mustache.

Finally, he speaks. "Together, it's obvious. Two very different girls. But apart? You are just alike enough to fool us silly, too-busy, know-it-all grown-ups, eh? Very clever."

"But, Morty." Esther stands, protesting. "We didn't switch with the purpose of fooling."

"No," Shira joins Esther in pleading their case. "We're good kids. It's just that Esther wants to study Torah. She needs to raise her voice to God."

"That's a noble thing," says Morty, crossing his arms and raising his eyebrows.

"And Shira," says Esther, "is so talented she wants—no, she *has*—to try out for the *Nicky Sanders Show*. The audition is on Sunday, and let's be honest—the stage needs *her*."

"Well, thanks, Ess!" Shira pops up to do a funny curtsy. "Even if Papa doesn't understand, it's my calling. And talk about calling!" She shakes her head and gestures to Esther. "I've never met someone so devoted to their faith." Esther bows her head.

Morty cleans his glasses and puts them back on his face, seeing each girl clearly. The girls grab each other's hands and hold tight. *Please don't tell*, they project, like the lingering clang of a trolley bell. If Morty reveals their swapped identities, Esther won't get to finish her bat mitzvah speech. Or say her portion. Or even lead tonight's Shabbat prayers.

Shira crosses the fingers on each hand and wishes she could cross her toes. She finally got the kick–ball change sequence of the dance. Would she ever get to perform it?

"So other than Benjamin, does anyone else know?"

They all shake their heads. "You won't tell, will you, Morty?"

Morty docsn't answcr right away. Finally, hc spcaks. "Anyone asks? I don't know nothin'." He lifts his hands to the heavens. "I'm just a deli man."

CHAPTER EIGHTEEN

SHABBAT SHALOM

ESTHER SPENDS THE TROLLEY ride back to the rabbi's house trying to think like Shira. She considers how to best set the scene so he'd believe *she* made the challah and knishes, not me, Morty. Her costume? A cooking apron on top of the single dress Esther has in her closet. Props? Mixing bowls, cups, and spoons in the drying rack. Expression? Exhausted—as if she'd been baking in a hot kitchen all day.

Speaking of thinking like Shira, she couldn't believe that she—a book person—didn't consider that the numbers on the menu might correspond to a book page. Sure enough, on the far bottom right of the second bookcase in the living room, sandwiched between the side of the case and a book called *Keeping a Jewish Home*, she finds *Jewish Cookery*, by Leah Leonard.

Sitting cross-legged on the floor, she flips to the index. After the *blintzes*, *challah*, and *knaidlach*, but before the *kreplach* and *kugel*, is the word *knish*. Esther exhales and checks the page—253. She laughs at how difficult it is to be someone she's not. She laughs at the codes and patterns and traditions that make each family a family.

She flips to page 253 and reads. The potato-y inside of the knish is made separately from the fluffy outside doughy part, then they're put together and baked. Her eyes land on the long list of ingredients: oil, salt, pepper, onion, potato, egg, parsley, water, *shmaltz*, flour. "Holy knish."

Shira knows how to do this? Esther shakes her head. She remembers the catastrophe that was her baked chicken and boiled potatoes and is relieved and happy that Benny picked up the challah and knishes from the deli, even if it did mean that I found out that she and Shira switched places. She's relieved that at least one grown-up knows where she is, I'm sure of it.

As Esther lets the pages fan closed, she hears the trolley bell clang far away and feels a tingle course through her arms and spine. "That was odd," she says. When she looks down, the inscription at the front of the book stares back.

To my darling sister Mona on her wedding day. May your home be a haven of peace. Love, MC. Uncle Coop's first name begins with an *M*? Esther thinks about the photo on the rabbi's desk. Did he look familiar because he looked like Shira . . . or because he looks like *her*?

Mayne kinder. This may seem like a big leap. *M* could stand for anything: *Mitchell, Milton, Macabee.* But it could also stand for *Mel.* Let's face it, only one letter in the alphabet could. If she could see the back of the photo in the rabbi's office, perhaps she could discover Uncle Coop's first name—and wouldn't that explain some things.

Before the congregants arrive at the synagogue, Esther and the rabbi put out prayer books, they get the wine and challah ready, they spread tablecloths in the community room. There isn't a moment without the rabbi. There isn't a moment to sneak away to look at the photograph.

As she and Rabbi Epstein wait on the synagogue steps for the carts of people from Scheinfeld's to arrive, Rabbi Epstein straightens Esther's *tallis* and holds her face in his hands. "You are a blessing," he tells her.

Oh, my aching heart! She wants to accept this blessing, but she knows it is meant for Shira. Where is her own father? She wishes *he* could come to her bat mitzvah next week.

The hum and rattle of golf carts on the small dirt road that connects the resort to the synagogue interrupt all her thoughts of Mel and bring her back to the moment. *Please don't let me flub the prayers. Please let them think I'm Shira.* She runs through the blessings in her head. *Barukh atah Adonai . . .*

It's a good thing that most of the summer congregants are from the Scheinfeld's Resort and Cottages instead of the town of Idylldale. Because the resort guests come and go from week to week, Esther is forgiven if she seems to forget a name or two. Thankfully, standing next to the rabbi is a quick way to learn names. The first woman to mount the stairs has a straw hat that looks like a flattened cinnamon bun. "Mrs. Goldberg, so lovely to see you," Rabbi

Epstein says, so Esther knows to say, "Good Shabbos, Mrs. Goldberg."

Or the rabbi says, "Shira, look who's here!" and Esther says, "It's wonderful to see you again! How's the family?" She finds that enthusiasm can take the place of intimacy and figures it is a pretty good bet that, whoever they are, everyone has some family somewhere.

One small boy asks for a joke. Luckily, Shira taught her one for just this occasion. "What do you call a crate of ducks?" she asks him.

He shrugs.

"A box of quackers!"

He stares at her sideways, and she knows Shira would have told it better. "Not every joke lands," she says, winking.

All of sudden he says, "Oh! Quackers, crackers!" He runs back to his parents and tells them the joke. Shira knows her audience.

Once the congregation is seated for Shabbat services, Esther tries to calm her butterflies. The butterflies tell her that in the past, she only *pretended* to celebrate Shabbat and that this is the real thing—a thing she should be nervous about. But *kinder*, doesn't the flame of a birthday candle bring as much warmth as that of a Shabbat candle? What is the difference between a prayer that is scripted and one that she offers from her heart? When will Esther realize that it is her *intention* when she lights the candle that defines her, not the flame itself?

She is on the rabbi's heels as he mounts the stairs to the raised platform that is the place of honor in the synagogue—the *bima*. She is so close that when he stops, she runs right into his legs.

"Sorry, Father," she says. "I'm nervous."

He hands her the matchbox. "Really? I thought you love speaking in public."

"I guess I care about it more now that we've been studying together."

He smiles, pats her cheek, and makes a space for her in front of the candles.

Esther takes a deep breath, runs through the beginning of the prayer in her head again, and exhales. The faces of the congregants are bathed in pink sunset, and she wishes—so badly—that her mother were among them. Wouldn't she be proud of her performing daughter now! She strikes the match. *Scratch, pop*—it bursts into flame.

In that flash are all of her dreams. As the candle wicks light, a glow spirals from deep inside and fills her. She stands before the rabbi and pulls the light of the candles into her, once, twice, three times. The warmth swirls against her face and becomes part of her essence and being. She covers her eyes.

And then it's happening. The blessing that Shira taught her at the Trolley Transfer Station, her voice—her familiar, regular voice; *Esther's own voice*—floats around the dome of the synagogue as she blesses the candles.

As she chants, her mind feels free. She lets it wander, lets it land on the most marvelous part of her life, the part that led her to this stage right now: She and Shira were born on the same day in the same place. In her blessing is thanks for the miracle of her world and Shira's world and how they had been connected, then somehow were separated, and then, miraculously, had collided once again. Always entwined. Even if Benny hadn't brought them together,

Esther thinks in the silence after the blessing, they would have found each other somehow. It was meant to be. She feels sure of it.

All these feelings, she puts into her prayer. And it feels both unbelievable and perfectly right at the same time.

Slowly, she opens her eyes and looks to the rabbi. His head is tilted as if he's seeing her for the first time, and she's struck with the impulse to tell him, right now, who she is. But: *Beautiful*, he mouths, and the love inside Esther, as bright as the flames near her face, illuminates the place inside her that felt fatherless, the place that felt not-Jewish-enough. She wants this feeling to last forever. "Thank you, Shira," says Rabbi Epstein. "Please be seated."

At the end of the service, Frank and his wife bring out small paper cups of wine for the adults and grape juice for the children. Esther blesses the wine and the challah bread flawlessly, and when everyone else retires to the community room, she stays in the sanctuary a little longer.

Touching the covered mole on her neck, her fingers come away tinted with makeup, but she rubs her hands and the color fades. Is she fading into Shira, or growing into a new Esther?

As she passes Rabbi Epstein's office on the way to join the others, the photo frame on his desk draws her in like Fanny to a spotlight. Slipping inside, she remembers the rabbi's pronouncement: *The only time when a child should question their parent is when the parent keeps him or her from studying the Torah.* Well, this isn't that. She knows she is disobeying. Then again, Rabbi Epstein isn't actually her father, so maybe the Torah portion doesn't apply to this situation.

At the rabbi's desk, she picks up the frame and examines Uncle Coop again. He has round glasses and a handsome, wide smile. His slicked-back hair is tucked behind his ears, his nose has a small bump at the bridge, and his chin is shaped with a tiny divot she didn't notice before. She rubs her own nose, her chin. The same. She looks at Mrs. Epstein and back to the man. Behind his glasses, they have the same eyes—the same eyes that she and Shira share too.

With trembling hands, she opens the small tabs that keep the backing on the frame. She lifts it. There *is* writing on the photo.

Mona Cooper Epstein and Samuel Epstein at the
birth of their daughter, Shira Epstein. With Mel
Cooper, Uncle Coop!

Uncle Coop's first name *is* Mel. If he is *her* Mel, that would make Esther and Shira cousins. No wonder they look so similar!

"Shira Ruth?"

Esther startles and fumbles, the frame flies into the air, hits the hard floor, and glass shatters—the photo fluttering down. Rabbi Epstein, wide-eyed, bends to rescue the photo from the shards just as Esther does the same, and there is a sickening *rip*. Each of them ends up with half of the photo.

"What . . . did . . . you . . . do?" the rabbi whispers, astonished.

When Fanny is angry, she is like a full balloon that you've let go, spitting guilt this way and that. "How could you do this to *me*," Fanny cried when Esther spilled makeup on Fanny's costume. "Think of your *mother*," Fanny moaned when Esther put dinner for the whole crew on their tab at the deli. Because she's lived with Fanny for almost thirteen years, Esther knows what makes Fanny angry and knows how to exist within those boundaries.

But this man. This father. Samuel Epstein? Esther doesn't know how he will react. "I just meant to look . . ."

He shakes his head and sucks his finger.

"Are you hurt?" she says stepping closer, but he steps away.

"*Gey avek*," he says, his words as sharp as the splintered glass in his finger. For Esther, Yiddish is usually comforting, but never before has she been told to *go away*.

"I'm so sorry," she whispers. Esther backs out of the rabbi's office as silently as one might back away from an angry grizzly, sure that making a sound will make the bear angrier.

In the hallway, Esther can hear the tinkle of glass fragments falling into the garbage can. She buries her face in her hands and slides down the wall.

Ah, sweet *kinder*. Sometimes we do things we know we shouldn't do, and it hardly ever turns out well. One time, I bit a knish that was just out of a piping-hot oven. My tongue was so burned. How burned? So burned, I couldn't taste anything else for a week.

Esther knew she shouldn't have gone into the rabbi's office, but she did. She knew the photo was the only one of its kind, and she opened the frame anyway. Now Rabbi Epstein is hurt, the frame is broken, and the photo . . . Half of the photo, *kinder*, is in her hand. The guilt is overwhelming. She looks at it again through pooling tears. On the front—the man who shares her eyes, chin, and the bump on the bridge of her nose. On the back—the name, *Mel Cooper*. She wipes her eyes. Where is her father now?

Just then Rabbi Epstein appears in the doorway with an extended hand, his eyes averted. She places her half of the photo in his palm, and both the rabbi and Mel disappear once again.

CHAPTER NINETEEN

AUDITION DAY

A SCHEINFELD'S BELLHOP HOLDS the glass doors for Shira and Fanny on audition day. Before they can enter the lush lobby, three matching kids wearing mini bow ties shove around their skirts with their mother in hot pursuit. "Boys! Apologize to the nice lady."

"Sor-ry," they say in unison.

Fanny stage-whispers to Shira, "Should I tell them I'm not a nice lady?"

Shira giggles nervously. She has often been to Scheinfeld's with her father to meet synagogue donors or young couples planning their weddings, so she's seen the chandelier with crystal shades blooming from gold branches that crowns the grand lobby. What she hasn't seen was Scheinfeld's looking like this: girls in tutus climbing over the floral brocade sofas; a toddler in a fancy wing chair wearing lederhosen, swinging his legs, and eyeing a large lollipop; a pigtailed girl with a bow and quiver full of arrows standing at the front desk. Each of them has a parent who hopes this audition might make their child a star.

Fanny, who has never before allowed Esther to visit Scheinfeld's, assumes her daughter is admiring the luxury of the resort. Shira plays her part—*ooh*-ing and *ahh*-ing at all the fancy finishings. She even throws in a question or two before she hears Benny call into the din.

"Excuse me." No one else hears him. "May I have your attention? Please?"

Nothing.

Fanny sticks her thumb and middle finger into her mouth and sends up a piercing whistle. The main lobby falls silent, and Benny winks his thanks at Fanny.

"All families here for the Nicky Sanders auditions, please take the curved staircase and follow the signs down to the ballroom."

And away they bustle, children of all shapes and sizes in colorful costumes with a variety of instrument cases and props. While the families file away, Benny slips in beside Shira and squeezes her arm gently. "You doing okay?"

"My *kishkes* are in an uproar," she whispers, holding her belly. And of course Shira's tummy is upset! Not only is she about to audition for a celebrity she adores, but she also wants to impress Fanny.

"You'll be fine. You've been practicing nonstop. Breathe, and your stomach will feel better in plenty of time—Nicky Sanders is known for being fashionably late."

Fanny swoops up. "Of course he is. He'll want to make an entrance," she says, and mutters, "he always has."

"Lots of kids here," Shira says. For the first time, her confidence has taken a hit. "I might not get this."

"Nonsense, *bubbele*. You're gonna be great. You're the daughter of Red. Hot. Fanny."

Shira, *not*-the-daughter-of-Red-Hot-Fanny, gulps.

No one likes to wait, but *azoy iz es*, so it is. As hard as you try, sitting still turns to squirmy and squirmy turns to wiggly. The staff of Scheinfeld's tries to make the delay better with crackers, juice, and fruit, but food does not help Shira's nerves. Instead, she paces the back of the room, cracker crumbs crunching underfoot. When she slips on an errant grape, she grabs for someone to steady her and looks up to find . . . Nicky Sanders himself.

"Whoa, careful there, cutie. When we say, 'break a leg,' we don't really mean it."

Do you remember Shira's room, with its many posters of Nicky Sanders's smile? Now Shira is face-to-face with that smile, and she couldn't be more tongue-tied. "Mr. Sanders, I . . . You . . . I mean . . . Oh my, you're even more handsome in real life!" Shira slaps her hand over her mouth, but it's too late. She's already said it, and her face is as red as a bowl of Rose Morgenstern's borscht.

Nicky Sanders flashes his pearly whites, makes sure that Shira is steady, and gives a little up-nod to the man and woman behind him. The woman reaches into her tote bag and pulls out a signed photo. Shira takes it without mentioning that she's already got five others just like it.

As Miss Scheinfeld approaches, the realization of possible discovery hits like a falling theater curtain. Shira ducks her head and covers her face with her hand, but Miss Scheinfeld sweeps by. "This way, Mr. Sanders," she says and Nicky Sanders follows her to the front of the ballroom. "We've set up the table by the stage just as you requested. There's seltzer water, and a Reuben with extra sauerkraut."

Nicky Sanders looks at the plate of food, and silence blankets the crowd. "Ah, dear Miss Scheinfeld. You've forgotten the most important snack of all. My Nibbles chips! And why Nibbles, girls and boys?" His voice booms playfully over the crowd and they all sing back:

"Because we've got no quibbles
with the crispy, crunchy,
always need to munch a
chiiip caaalled Nibbles."

Fanny raises her eyebrows at Shira, who has joined the advertisement jingle sing-along. "You know he shills for that company because they pay him, right?"

"It's a catchy jingle," Shira says, defending herself.

"All right, boys and girls. Now that I've got your attention, let me introduce you to the lovely Miss Hayes, who will tell you what to expect. And this is our accompanist, Mr. Blum."

Mr. Blum is a rumpled man with a round nose in the middle of round cheeks and a flop of hair combed over a round head. He takes a microphone from the stage, and feedback echoes through the hall. Dozens of children clap their hands over their ears. "Sorry," he says and jogs up the stage stairs. "We'll move this along just as quickly as we can, folks. We'll call ten numbers at a time. When you hear your number, line up stage right and hand me your sheet music."

"That's over here," Miss Hayes points.

"Right. Stage right is your left," Mr. Blum says, and Shira blows away some of her worry. At least she already knows her stage left from her stage right.

Miss Hayes is on the stage now, and she takes the microphone. She is as vogue and vertical as Mr. Blum is rumbled and round. Her collar is buttoned to her neck, and her knee-skimming, narrow skirt looks professional and smart. She has an upturned nose and a smile that would be just right on a kindergarten teacher. "There are a lot of talented children here," she says kindly. "But remember, while we wish we could celebrate you all, we only need five acts for the on-air contest. If you aren't chosen, just know that we are looking for acts that work well with live television. Sometimes that's not the same as what works on the stage. That doesn't mean you aren't wonderful," she assures them. "We just need to know that you can perform to a camera."

"So if we say *no thank you*, please don't argue," Mr. Blum says, taking the microphone back. "I can't tell you the number of times that some upset mother has found me in the parking lot and—"

"Mr. Blum," Miss Hayes cuts him off and reclaims the mic. "Kids, I'll be at stage left with candy and an autographed photo for each of you. So really, you're all winners! Remember, Mr. Sanders is *so* glad you're here . . . and he asked me to tell you"—she bends down and gets quiet, like she has a secret—"that his book *Keep 'Em Laughing* is for sale at the hotel gift shop. Now, numbers 1 through 10, you can line up."

Shira looks at her number. Thirty-six. "Double *chai*," she says. "That's good luck."

Fanny grips Esther's chin and stares into her eyes. Then she tilts her head and wrinkles her brow. For a moment, Esther thinks she's been discovered, but Fanny just kisses her on the cheek. The shadow of lipstick Fanny leaves behind is warm and wonderful, like a birthday candle.

"You don't need lucky numbers, my girl," Fanny says and wipes off the lipstick. "You've got talent."

Unlike the lipstick, Fanny's words are as permanent as the stars in the sky.

CHAPTER TWENTY

ESTHER VISITS ROSE

WHILE SHIRA WAITS FOR her audition, Esther marches through the Idylldale Hospital, her wrist stiff from writing twenty-five times, "To everything there is a season." A time to be silly, a time to be serious. A time to be in Rabbi Epstein's office, a time to stay out. While it was Esther's first time being punished, she had the feeling that it was not Shira's. To be honest, Esther would have written the lines twenty-five more times if it would have eliminated the shame she felt from ripping that photo.

Now the rabbi opens Rose Morgenstern's door, and Esther thinks, *This is definitely a time to be serious.* She goes right up to Rose and grasps the old woman's hand in her two as she imagines a good Rabbi's Daughter might—with empathy and kindness. "How are you *feeling*?" she asks seriously.

Rabbi Epstein and Rose turn to her abruptly. "*Nu?*" says Rose. "I expect jokes from you, not sympathy."

"Well," the rabbi explains, "Shira is trying to make a change. She is about to become a bat mitzvah, you know. To become someone else—a young woman, in the eyes of the congregation."

"Someone else, you say." Rose looks deep into Esther's eyes. "Then she is succeeding. Have you heard, Rabbi, that Nicky Sanders is coming to town? In fact, the auditions are today."

Esther pulls her hand away from Rose, drops her eyes, and picks at her thumbnail.

"Yes. Miss Scheinfeld is very excited about the publicity it will bring to her resort," says the rabbi. "She told me at the social after services. Oh, and Rose. Shira did a wonderful job at Shabbat services. I've never seen her so dedicated to her faith!"

"You don't say," Rose murmurs suspiciously.

"We had knishes at the *oneg*. Oh, I should have brought you one," Esther blathers. She's got a sneaky feeling Rose has got a sneaky feeling that something isn't as it seems.

"Anything would be better than what they feed you in here," Rose says. "The food here is *so* bad . . ."

Now at this point, as you know, any self-respecting comic performer would know to say, "How bad is it?" I've told you: This is a classic joke setup. Rose knows it. Shira knows it. Esther knows it too, but what she doesn't know is that this is the one room in the hospital where jokes, Shira's jokes specifically, are expected. A time to be silly, one might say. Her seriousness has been a grave miscalculation. Get it? *Grave* means "serious."

But Esther says nothing. She leaves Rose hanging. Now the rabbi might be grateful for some peace and quiet from his daughter, but for Rose, all her principal senses are tingling. She knows something, as we say, isn't kosher.

"Rabbi," Rose says, "would you be so kind as to get an old lady some water?"

Trying to be helpful, Esther tries to rise for the pitcher at Rose's bedside, but Rose—who, despite her illness, has a grip like a vise—yanks Esther back to her seat. "Rabbi. Some *fresh* water please? The pitcher is stale."

As soon as the door closes behind him, Rose tightens her grip on Esther's wrist. "What have you done with my Shira?"

She knows.

Esther pulls away and her eyes follow her hand into her lap again. "What do you mean? I am Shira."

"You think I'm *meshuge*? How you fooled Shira's own father is beyond me."

"But, Rose," Esther tries.

"Don't 'but Rose' me. If you're Shira, what was the last joke you told me?"

Esther racks her brain. All she knows is the one about the duck. "The box of quackers joke?"

"No!" Rose scoffs. "You must have been seven years old the last time you told me that baby joke." She shakes her head. "It was the one about the ill-fitting suit. Now spill. Who are you?"

First Morty, now this? Esther's hands are back on Rose's, pleading. "Are you going to tell? You can't tell. Shira is fine.

We've switched places so she can try out for Nicky Sanders today."

Rose's face goes from worry to wonder in an instant. "What? Me tell? I'm so happy for Shira I could *plotz*. Finally getting to audition! Such a performer." Then she pauses. "But who are you?"

Esther might break out into song and dance right here. She had no idea Rose would be so supportive. "I'm Esther Rosenbaum. Fanny Rosenbaum's daughter."

"*Oy.* Talk about *meshuge*. That Frances was always cutting up in class."

"Shira said you used to be the high school principal. So my mother was your student."

"Idylldale is big, but it's not New York City." Rose makes a circular gesture around Esther's face. "So how did this happen? You do look awfully similar."

"I might be Shira's cousin." Then it's Esther's turn to pause. "But don't tell her! She doesn't know yet."

Rose leans forward. "Tell me more." Esther looks over her shoulder at the door, but Rose waves away her worry. "I happen to know that Mr. Aaronson is in his last days, which means the rabbi will be at the nurse's station for a while. We've got time."

So Esther tells the whole story: Benny introducing them, learning her Torah portion with the rabbi, Shira rehearsing with Fanny, the inscription in the cookbook. She shows Rose the dimple in her chin and tells her how Shira, Esther, Mona, and Mel all share the same eyes. She confesses to ripping the photo with *Mel Cooper* on the back and ends with the part about how Mel somehow made it to Shira's birth but couldn't be bothered to be at her own—his own daughter's. "And he's never once tried to get in touch with me!" She hears the sadness in her voice as she tells her sad truth.

Rose takes a deep breath, so deep it rattles in her chest. "Perhaps our dear Fanny never told him about you."

Esther doesn't expect this. For so long, she didn't have a real story about her father, so she had made up her own. *Once upon a time, there was a baby whose father didn't want her, so he left. The baby tried to learn everything she could and make everything as perfect as she could, so that if her father, one day, came back, he would want her.*

But if the father in her story never even knew about her? Well, then all that she'd told herself was untrue.

"And if he didn't know about the pregnancy, he wouldn't have any reason to believe she'd be in the hospital at all, much less that same day. All his thoughts would be on his sister, don't you think?"

A lump forms in Esther's throat and her eyes well up with tears. Why would her mother have kept her existence a secret from her own father? She thinks of their bedtimes. About all the secrets they share when the lights are out. Sometimes, it feels as if Fanny is her sister and not her mother. She has to admit, her mother is exactly the type to decide she could raise a child all by herself without any help. "Never told him?" Her imagined history shatters like the glass from the picture frame. She wipes her cheeks.

"Maybe Mel didn't come back to the Heights because he thought it was just a normal breakup. Fanny was always a heartbreaker." Rose pats Esther's hand. "And maybe she had no idea she was pregnant when he left."

"But what about Shira?" Esther sniffs. "Why wouldn't Mel at least come to see his niece after the birth? He was in that picture. He knows *she* exists."

"Who says he doesn't? It sounds as if you haven't asked her or the rabbi."

"No," Esther agrees. She had tried to figure out everything all by herself. "I guess I thought if he came to see Shira that he'd see Fanny. And know about me."

"Not necessarily. New York it isn't, but Idylldale is no small town. He could be here to visit Shira and never go near the Heights. Just think, you'd never been to the synagogue yourself until you switched!" Rose holds up one crooked finger. "And I don't know Mel, but if he really loved your mother *body and soul*, as you say, I'm sure that, one, he was devastated by their breakup and, two, he'd love you just as much."

"I Iuh." Esther sits back to think. "But what if . . ."

"If, if. If my grandmother had wheels and flies, she'd be a garbage truck. Why don't you ask Mel yourself?"

Esther feels hope jump into heart like guests dancing the hora at a wedding. "Do you know him?!"

"No, but you know someone who does." Rose moves her crooked finger to her lips, and Esther shushes as the rabbi enters. "So smart, this girl of yours, Rabbi. She could do anything she sets her mind to. And now, I need some rest. God willing, I'll see you next Saturday at your ceremony."

"Are you sure, Rose? I'm happy to stay a bit longer," says the rabbi.

"No, no." Now Rose is drifting off to sleep.

"Mrs. Morgenstern is tired, Father," Esther says, pulling him away. But when she takes one last look over her shoulder, Rose Morgenstern is giving her a thumbs-up.

CHAPTER TWENTY-ONE

THE AUDITION

THE RABBI, NEEDING TO counsel Mr. Aaronson's family, sends Esther home to study, and does she listen? No, she does not. She goes directly to Scheinfeld's.

Esther sneaks from shady tree to scratchy bush until she sees Benny loading a car with luggage. She waits for him to slap the top of the car twice before she calls, "Ben!"

"Esther!" He jumps. "You can't be here."

"I have to see Shira's audition. Please, Benny."

"This way," he says, his eyes flashing with welcome mischief. "I have an idea." He takes her hand and they jog down the path that Esther walked a week ago. Today, though, they duck into a dark green metal EMPLOYEES ONLY door.

This hall has more in common with the sterile hallways of the hospital than the guest halls with lush red carpeting and pleasant recorded music. Other hotel workers bustle past, and the chug of washing machines matches their pace as their feet squeak on the linoleum. Steamy heat engulfs them. When the hall takes a sharp turn to the left, Benny calls, "This way," and the clatter of dishes gets louder.

"Hey, Moishe!" Benny shouts. "I need to grab a cart."

"No problem, Benny!" Moishe shouts from the dishwashing room.

"Get in," he tells Esther, and he lifts the white linen cloth draped over the room service cart. He offers her a hand as if she's a fancy lady stepping into a limousine.

Our rule-following Esther doesn't even argue; she just settles into the tiny space. "I feel like a dog trapped in a kennel," she laughs.

"No barking," Benny says. He zips the cart through the hallways and positions it in the back of the ballroom. If Esther parts the flaps of the tablecloth, she can see the stage. It's like her own personal theater curtains! And look! There's Fanny in the audience.

For twelve years Esther had never been far from her home and the Heights. Now, she hasn't slept in her own bed or seen her mother for almost a week. She wants to crawl out of her hiding spot and throw her arms around Fanny's neck, but just then Nicky Sanders calls out, "Esther Rosenbaum. Number 36?"

Shira raises a hand and calls out, "That's me!" while Esther, under the cart, whispers the same thing.

Shira has her umbrella, a yellow overcoat and hat, and red rain boots. As planned, she also has on various layers that she'll take off with the proper words of the song. But Nicky Sanders has other ideas before the music starts up. "Rosenbaum?" he asks. "Any relation to Fanny Rosenbaum?"

"She's my mother," Shira says, feeling proud of how naturally the lie rolls off her tongue, and all eyes follow her point to the back of the room.

And will you look at that? Fanny waves at Nicky. Not a friendly whole-hand wave like the nurses at the hospital, or a languorous parade-queen wave, but a flirty with-her-fingers-only kind of wave. Shira doesn't know what that means, but Esther (under the cart) sniffs it out: Fanny and

Nicky have crossed paths before, and there may have even been some kissing involved. She's seen her mother like this many a time. And under the cart, Esther rolls her eyes.

"Nicky, darling. Long time no see."

"Red. Hot. Fanny," he replies, and even with all those children in the room, there is a moment of awkward silence.

Esther (you know where) buries her blushing face in her hands. There was definitely kissing.

Miss Hayes coughs. "Mr. Blum," she says, "shall we proceed?"

"We shall, Miss Hayes," Mr. Blum says. "'Button Up Your Overcoat' in G? I don't need the music," he says when Shira tries to hand it to him. "It's one of my favorites. Break a leg." Shira runs up the stairs and stands at center stage.

Miss Hayes speaks from stage left. "No need to be nervous, Esther. We just want to see what you can do."

Fanny gives her a thumbs-up from the back row and mouths, *From the diaphragm*, to encourage Shira to sing out strong.

As the first bars of the introduction play, to Shira, the stage feels like home.

When you use a toaster, *kinder*, you push a lever and the bread goes down. It heats and heats until, *pop*, it jumps out as toast. The toast is still bread, but it's different—golden brown. This is what being onstage feels like for Shira. The music, the stage, and now the audience warm her from the inside out. She is the same, but different. And when she opens her mouth, *pop*—her voice is golden.

At the beginning of the second verse, Esther (still squashed under the room service cart) worries that Nicky Sanders will hold up his hand, stop the audition, and dismiss Shira despite her beautiful voice. She has seen plenty of directors dismiss great performers from auditions at the Heights because they weren't *right for the part.* She glances at her mother, whose hands are together as if they're in prayer, mouthing the words to the song and wiggling, doing the routine in her own seat. If she were any happier, she'd be a purring cat.

She thinks that's me, and for a moment, Esther imagines herself up there on the stage. Would Fanny look at her in the same way? Would Esther even want that?

No, she would not. What Esther wants is for Fanny to glow for Esther's love of Torah study. *If I were up there,*

Esther thinks, *I'd just be going through the motions to please Mama.*

Shira, on the other hand, isn't thinking at all. She's a performer performing. She doesn't think about the outcome of the audition or being discovered as an imposter. She is transported away from herself, and at the same time, she is the most *Shira* she's ever been. On that stage it is Shira and the hours and hours of practice that have made the dance steps second nature.

Shira leans into some silly faces, and the audience answers by laughing. They're tapping their toes too. After this audition, Shira will realize she was wrong to compare her father's services to the theater. In their synagogue, the congregation is scripted. In the theater, though, there is a conversation with the audience, and their reactions are unexpected. She sings. She dances. She *is* joy.

But then! What's happening? *Drip, drip.* Real water shocks her as it pings against her cheek and her head, but it's the third chorus, so Shira keeps on singing. *Drizzle, drizzle.* Now a stream of water threatens to muffle her voice, but she won't let it close her throat in fear. She keeps the raincoat on (not choreographed), opens her umbrella (choreographed), sings from the diaphragm, and drowns out the increasing *pitter-patter* all around her. After all, how many times did Fanny tell her *the show must go on?*

In the audience, when the drips become a drizzle, Esther watches Miss Hayes abandon her post at stage left and tugs on Benny's pant leg. "Over there," she says to Benny. "Follow Miss Hayes."

Benny does. He casually rolls the cart to the doorway where Miss Hayes and Miss Scheinfeld are whisper yelling.

"You promised us a luxury venue! Why is there water pouring from the ceiling?"

Miss Scheinfeld's smile is as tight as a stretched rubber band. "We are eager to make this right and look forward to hosting the live telecast."

"You'll host *bupkes* if this can't be fixed," Miss Hayes declares, her kindergarten-teacher kindness replaced with firm authority.

"Benjamin, call Frank right now."

"Yes, Ma'am!" Benny says, and pulls out his beloved two-way radio.

"This is Frank." It's a familiar voice shouting over a familiar sound: a whining vacuum. Esther and Miss Scheinfeld hear him too.

"Frank, it's Benny Bell. There's a . . . plumbing situation in the main ballroom."

Ah, Frank knows everything there is to know about water pipes, but right now he's tending to another crisis, eyeing the glint of glass in the fibers of the rabbi's carpet. "Can it wait?"

Onstage, even in the middle of the plumbing-induced downpour, Shira is smiling. "Well . . . maybe?" says Benny.

Miss Scheinfeld grabs the walkie-talkie and fumbles with the button. "Frank. This is Debra Scheinfeld. There's water everywhere! I need you. Now!"

At the synagogue, Frank drops his vacuum and hurries out the door.

In the ballroom, Shira finishes in a growing puddle, giving one last happy stomp-kick that sprays the water in an arc around her. She holds her final position under the umbrella, even though she just danced her heart out. With water above and water below, she shines with accomplishment, and the audience shines right back. It's enough to make a rainbow!

Fanny sticks two fingers in her mouth and whistles.

Benny cheers.

Even Nicky Sanders gives her a standing ovation. "Now that's performing under pressure!" he says.

The whole ballroom is going wild. Listen! Good thing they're too loud to notice Esther clapping under that cart.

CHAPTER TWENTY-TWO

SHPILKES

ESTHER WATCHES TOMATO SOUP swirl in the pot as she
stirs. Tomato soup is easy—open the can, pour it in the pot,
turn on the burner, and ta-da—soup. You know what isn't
easy? Love, and the situation these girls are in.

When Shira performed, Fanny glowed as if she had just
sipped warm soup. Did that mean that she loved Shira more
than Esther? Of course not. In fact, Fanny thought the pride
she felt *was* for her own daughter. She thought that it was
Esther up there truly having fun, and she was certain that
the fun was what made the performance so good. Just the

same: When Esther lit the candles during Shabbat, the rabbi's pride was for Shira.

This is all so complicated. Less like soup and more like a grilled cheese sandwich. Let's say one slice of bread is Fanny and the other one is the rabbi, and Esther and Shira are the cheese in the middle. Just like the bread keeps the cheese nestled and safe so it can melt no matter how hot the griddle gets, these parents want to love and protect their children. What? Too much with the food metaphors? Maybe, but can you blame me? I'm a deli man.

The point is, if Rabbi Samuel Epstein and Fanny Rosenbaum finally saw Shira and Esther finding joy in their passions, they would glow for their own children. Of this, I'm as sure as the taste of grilled cheese dipped in tomato soup. Complicated, but delicious.

Also complicated is the rabbi's dinner table where the only sound is the occasional *tink* of spoon on soup bowl and a subsequent *slurp*. Two days have passed since the ripped-photo disaster, and Esther has been very careful to be on her best behavior.

Now, waiting for the audition results in the evening newspaper, it is difficult for Esther to be still and quiet. She's all motion. She squirms under the rabbi's indifferent gaze. She wiggles while waiting, and she startles when the paper hits the door. "Can I get that?" she asks.

"If it'll cure your *shpilkes*." *Shpilkes*. Isn't that a great Yiddish word? It means jumpy and restless—like you've got ants in your pants. Quick as a wink, Esther's at the door. She flicks open page after page until she finds the list of five acts that have made it on to the *Nicky Sanders Show*. "She got it!"

"Who got what?" the rabbi says, dipping his grilled cheese sandwich in tomato soup.

"Shira—" Esther says.

"Shira? You?"

Esther glances at the rabbi and shakes the paper open in front of her face as she sits. "No, *she* . . . *hoorah!*" It's not a good lie; she doesn't have much practice, but Rabbi Epstein has already taken a section of the paper and moved on. Esther continues. "My friend . . . um, Esther, got into the *Nicky Sanders Show!*"

"Again with that Nicky Sanders show," the rabbi says. "I've told you before, young people shouldn't be involved in show business." He sips from his teacup as if that is that.

Esther knows he's still upset. She knows she should follow the advice of her Torah portion and honor his feelings. But she—her real Esther self—has been in show business since she was born, and not only has she turned out fine so far, but she also took pride in Shira's performance joy. If she was on pins and needles before, now it seems her chair is made of nails. "Papa, how can you say that? Don't you want me on the *bima* with you, in front of the congregation? That's a performance too."

"We've discussed this. We do what we do in synagogue not as performers but as leaders of faith, for a larger purpose. Not for ourselves, but for the community and in service to God." He looks at her sharply, and Esther sees that his brief patience is gone. "You may be excused."

Esther is done with her soup and sandwich, but she is not done with this conversation. She plants herself next to the rabbi, their stacked dishes rattling along with her nerves.

Shira's past efforts to convince the rabbi to support her theatrical dreams have failed. Perhaps *this* is another reason why Esther is here now. Perhaps this is one of those *times*: a time to speak up. "What if," Esther says, "what if people in show business have a larger purpose beyond themselves too?" She wonders if this is true for her mother. She thinks, now, that it might be.

"Oh, come now." The rabbi returns his concentration to the paper.

"Maybe they want to bring joy to the audience, to relieve them of their pain and worry."

"Speaking of pain and worry." He puts down the paper. "I was at the hospital all day, and now I want a peaceful evening with my daughter. Not an argument. Not broken glass," he says pointedly. "Peace."

Esther puts the plate and bowl back on the table. "Maybe we should be more compassionate to people from all walks of life and honor all of God's many worlds." Shira's words to Esther from when they first met have never been truer.

Now, the rabbi stands and looks down his hawk nose at Esther. "That's enough from you, Shira Ruth Epstein." She crosses her arms to protect her heart. His voice booms. "Is your bat mitzvah speech done?"

"Um . . . No."

"Do you feel confident about your Hebrew?"

"Not . . . exactly."

"Tomorrow, you will finish your speech and study while I am at work. Our community is coming together for you in five days, and I will not be embarrassed. You'd think someone adult enough to read Torah wouldn't be so disrespectful." He shakes his head. "I'll see you in the morning."

Dishes in the sink, Esther hugs herself tighter, tucks her chin, and stomps up the stairs. At least Fanny never punished her for speaking her mind.

She throws a stuffed bear from the bed across the room, hitting the desk lamp, and grabs the toppling fixture just in time. Phew! She needed more broken glass *vi a lokh in kop*, like a hole in the head (which means she didn't need it at all). Etched on the lampshade are two parent rabbits and a baby bunny, and it's the first time she admits to herself what she wants—both Fanny and Mel (her father, her *real* father) glowing with pride at the bat mitzvah. But how could she get them there?

Esther reaches for the study folder on Shira's dresser and opens it to their bat mitzvah Torah portion. She thought that studying would always be joyful, but studying alone can be, well . . . lonely. How will she write a speech *and* figure out the things that Rabbi Epstein thinks she already knows, like the order of the service and taking the Torah from the ark? Her to-do list feels as heavy as a tube of kosher beef bologna.

Back at the Heights, the evening paper has yet to be delivered, so the young newsie and Shira and Fanny wait, both of them edging closer to the curb each time they hear a vehicle. Finally, the printer's truck turns the corner, and without stopping, a man throws a bundle of newspapers onto the sidewalk. The newsie cuts the string, takes Fanny's coin, and gives her the paper.

"What does it say, Mama? Am I in?" Shira watches as Fanny scans the front and rattles the pages, turning them one after the other until her face falls into a frown.

"No?" Shira asks.

Fanny flips her frown to a joyous grin. "Yes!"

They hook elbows and swing each other around until Shira screams in dizzy glee. The door to the Heights bangs open.

"What's wrong?" Levi's panic dissipates when he sees the smiles on their faces. "She made it?"

They both nod.

"She made it!" Bending down and extending his arms, Levi pats his strong shoulder, and Shira happily climbs aboard. They parade back and forth in front of the theater laughing and shouting, with Shira waving from her perch like a queen, until neighbors hang out of their windows clapping and cheering.

As soon as he lets her down, she jumps around, she skips, she hops, she wiggles her *tuchus* like the monkey in that infernal song. She's going to be on television competing for a thousand dollars!

On television. A stern voice slices through her celebration. *The entertainment business is no place for a child.* It is Papa's voice. Would he celebrate this moment?

She shakes his voice away and another one takes his place. Her own.

"Holy casserole," she shouts to the fire escapes. "I'm going to be on TV!"

CHAPTER TWENTY-THREE

SECRETS REVEALED

SHIRA HASN'T STOPPED SMILING since last night. After getting the good news, her dreams were full of theaters packed with audiences applauding for her. Now, with her hands over her eyes, her legs dangle off the edge of the stage. Her friends and family—Millie, Levi, Joshua, Benny, Fanny, and me, Morty—surround her, showering her with love and appreciation.

Well, *Esther's* friends and family. But who's to quibble?

"Okay. Open them!" Fanny says.

There, in her lap, is a shoebox with a bow. She tugs at the bow, and fawn-colored tap shoes with a small heel and crisscrossing straps nestle in tissue paper. Here is another dream fulfilled: new dance shoes to replace the too-small pair from her eighth birthday that she's kept in her closet at home.

She hugs the shoes close to her chest. "Oh, Mama, thank you, thank you!" she squeals. "They're just what I wanted!" She can hardly keep her hands from shaking as she slides on each one and buckles the straps.

She points.

She flexes.

She tries a few shuffles.

"I can take off the taps for you," Millie tells her.

"No. I want to learn more!"

"They're from the costume closet," Fanny explains. "I wish I could have gotten new, but . . ."

Shira reaches for Fanny and squeezes her tightly. "Mama, Millie, I love them. These are the best present ever."

"I'm so proud of you, Essie. The way you dealt with all that water!" Fanny shakes her head. "That's my girl!"

Shira cringes a little because, well, she isn't Fanny's girl at all. Nevertheless, Joshua nods, and Levi slaps the newspaper that he's been carrying around in his back pocket since they got the news last night.

"The show must go on," Shira says, and Fanny holds her cheeks and kisses her on the *keppie*.

Morty brought over the celebratory sandwiches himself. What a *mensch*! "But where'd the water come from?" he asks.

"A broken pipe," Benny explains. "The spa is right above the ballroom stage. Here's the thing, Frank the Handyman told Miss Scheinfeld they can't get the new parts before the actual *Nicky Sanders Show*."

Shira interrupts, "So that's when Mama tells Mr. Sanders—"

Fanny holds up her hands to stop both Shira and Benny. "So, that's when I tell Nicky . . . use. The. Heights."

A silence fills the theater as each of them surveys the shabby walls, curtains, chairs, and stage.

"Use the Heights? For the *Nicky Sanders Show*? The one that's supposed to celebrate Scheinfeld's? Televised live?" Levi asks.

"Yes! I spoke with him straight after the audition."

"You asked before you knew if Esther had gotten a slot?" Millie asks. "And what about the tears in the curtains?"

"Fanny," Levi lectures. "Do you know what goes into a television show? We'll need all new light bulbs in the spots. We can't afford that."

"That's exactly why I made this opportunity. You all should be thanking me! Nicky says that the network will take care of *all* the equipment needs. *This* is our way to fix up the Heights! For free!"

"*Nicky says*, does he?" Levi scoffs. "Remember how he offered you a place in the show before? Remember how he took it back when he found out you and Mel were expecting this little star?"

"He wasn't wrong. You can't take a baby on the road." She waves them away. "It's all water under the bridge. Showbiz."

"You think that was showbiz? *Feh.* He's a selfish man."

"Not the first. Not the last," Fanny says. "Anyway, when he told me that I'd be singing in the finale, of course I offered the Heights." She flings her arms above her, head tilted so the lights bathe her smile, one hip jutting out as if she'd just finished a big musical number. "It's the fate this theater has deserved for years!"

"Wait. We're going to be on TV together?"

"Won't that be fun, *bubbele*?"

"Sure," Shira says, but there's something about it that seems off. She thought Fanny wanted *Esther* to succeed. How did Fanny manage to tap-dance *herself* into the *Nicky Sanders Show*—without auditioning a single step?

Shira hugs everyone on their way out. "Congratulations, Esther," says Levi, the first to leave. "I got lots of dead bulbs to count."

Joshua chimes in, "Minna needs me at home. But congratulations, kid. I can say I knew you when."

Morty pats her shoulder. "You done good," he says, and gives her a wink.

Fanny and Millie disappear into the costume closet, promising to be right back.

And then it's just Shira and Benny. Shira takes a few bites of her sandwich in the quiet next to him. "You know Benny, I think she might be a little like my dad."

"Partly balding with a size 12 shoe?"

"Agh, no!" Shira's smile twitches, and she knocks her shoulder into Benny's. "No. More as if getting me on the show—"

"Getting *Esther* on the show."

"Right. Like that will be *her* success, not mine."

"And that's like the rabbi, how?"

"Like the bat mitzvah. I can count ten invitations we sent that *I* care about, and the rest are people from the community who don't even know me. It sometimes feels like he just wants to show me off."

"He is the rabbi of Idylldale. That doesn't seem odd."

"True," she says, talking through another bite. "But there's something else about Fanny and this show. Something that is odd, and I can't figure it out."

Benny shrugs. He eats his entire sandwich in one bite, jumps onstage, and starts practicing some routine before Shira realizes that neither Fanny nor Millie has returned. Behind her on the stage, Benny hops, holding his toe and crossing his eyes. "Ben. You look ridiculous."

"Of course I do. That's why it's funny."

Shira shrugs. "I'm going to find Mama."

Benny raises his eyebrows at her easy use of the word *Mama*.

I'll let you in on a secret, *mayne kinder*. In the past week, Shira has accepted Fanny criticizing her shorter hair because it meant that Fanny would also brush and style it. She has accepted long rehearsals because it meant that Fanny would bestow a short bit of praise now and again. She's accepted waking up with an elbow in her nostril because it meant she could fall asleep next to Fanny's gardenia and eucalyptus–scented skin. "Fanny, I mean. I'm going to find Fanny. Come with?"

Benny shrugs. "Okay."

They start down the stairs to the costume closet and freeze when they hear Fanny say, "Esther doesn't need to know." Shira was right. Something is up.

Shira presses her back to the wall and flattens Benny beside her. She holds a finger to her lips and slithers down a few more steps, curiosity coursing through her veins.

"She has a right to know," Millie says.

"It'll just put unnecessary pressure on her."

"She'll be fine. She's been doing so well."

"I see that," Fanny snaps. "But it's too much pressure, and we need her to win."

Benny and Shira make big eyes at each other. She scoots down one more step, trying to catch a glimpse of the two women, but an opened cupboard door hides Millie and most of Fanny.

"It's the only way I can think of to get enough money for Malaise."

Benny mouths, *Who's Malaise?* But Shira just shrugs.

"Face it, Frances. The people of Idylldale are done with nights at the Yiddish theater. They want stand-up comedians on televisions in their own homes." Millie clucks her tongue.

"I wish we'd said yes years ago when Alexander Malaise said he'd sell it to us."

"We didn't have the money then, Frances."

"No, and that's why we rent. But now, we don't even have the money for that. Come, we'll think better after we've eaten."

Benny's eyes grow big as bobbins and he points up the staircase. The two of them tiptoe up a few stairs and run the rest of the way—straight out of the theater.

Shira's brain is swirling with the bits and pieces she just heard. *Money. Sell. Alexander Malaise.* "Oh no," Shira says.

"What?"

"No, no, no. I totally forgot."

"What?"

"The day that we switched." She shakes her hands, trying to rid herself of the massive mistake she made. "There was a telegram from some guy named Alexander Malaise. We have to go!" Shira and Benny don't stop until they are in Fanny and Esther's fourth-floor apartment. "It's in the pocket of a skirt," she says, rushing to the clothes rod.

"Do you remember which one?"

"No." She looks in the pocket of each skirt and finds nothing. "But it's got to be here somewhere."

One skirt crinkles but it's a grocery list, not the telegram they need to find.

"Um . . . Laundry?"

She claps and points at Benny. "Yes!" She flips the hamper in the corner. "Help me, Ben."

"I don't want to touch Fanny's . . . um . . . unmentionables."

"Oh, please!"

Together they fling shirts, pants, socks, and unmention-ables aside, checking all pockets until, at the very bottom of the pile, they hear paper crinkle again.

She flattens the folded telegram and tears into it. Benny looks over her shoulder and they stare at the message together. "Oh, for the love of dogs and donkeys," she says.

TO: FRANCES ROSENBAUM

THE HEIGHTS THEATER

IDYLLDALE, NY

RENT OVERDUE—(STOP)—$1,500—(STOP)—THEATER TO BE

RAZED—(STOP)—PARKING LOT PLAN MOVING FORWARD—

(STOP)—BULLDOZERS ARRIVING NEXT FRIDAY MORNING—

(STOP)—REMOVE ANYTHING OF VALUE—(STOP)

FROM: ALEXANDER MALAISE

Shira is all agog. *Agog, mayne kinder*, is not a Yiddish word. It's English, and it means surprised or curious to hear something. "Benny, I . . ."

Fanny was right about the pressure of this new information. Before, Shira wanted to win. Now, she *has* to win, not for the five-city tour with the *Nicky Sanders Show* but for the money. She thinks about the rows and rows of red velvet seats and their obvious rips. "Benny, am I reading this right? Sounds like the theater will be a parking lot come Friday."

Fanny didn't trust Esther with this problem, and yet she's depending on Esther to solve it. Except the real Esther is as comfy in her new life as a guest at Scheinfeld's. Shira is on her own. What can she do to save the theater? She won her space on the *Nicky Sanders Show* by auditioning in a deluge. That won't happen during the live show. To win, her performance needs to be bigger. It needs to be better. And it's not as if she can invent a better bagel in a week.

But she can add in another bagel.

She can see it now, as if their names were up in lights: *Shira and Esther's Double Dream Debut!*

"Ben. Tell Esther we need another meeting."

CHAPTER TWENTY-FOUR

BENNY TO THE RESCUE

BENNY BELL KNOWS THAT if Shira and Esther try to meet at the Trolley Transfer Station again, the midpoint between the synagogue and the Heights, they could risk a run-in with another grown-up. Instead, he decides they'll use a place where there are grown-ups they can already trust.

The hospital elevator opens with a crisp *ding*, and Benny, put together in his bellboy's uniform with his hat in his hands, arrives on Rose Morgenstern's floor.

"May I help you, young man?" one of the nurses says.

Benny, silent, shows a wait-a-minute finger and evaluates the linoleum floor between them. It looks as if it might be wet and slick (even though it isn't) and he uses that for comedic effect. He takes a dramatically careful step—and in one quick moment he's flailing his long legs and arms. His feet are up, his *tuchus* is down, and his bellboy hat flies away from Rose Morgenstern's room. Instinctively, all three of the nurses pop to standing.

"Oh my, are you all right?" says the first nurse.

"Brilliant," says Shira, watching Benny's performance from the stairwell.

Benny just grins and flips over, palms on the ground, *tuchus* in the air, legs pumping behind him as if the floor is so slippery that he can't stand. He looks at his watch, as if he may have to do this all day, then at the concerned nurses. He crosses his eyes, and they laugh out loud. "He's like a comedian at Scheinfeld's," says the second.

"He's better than the comedian at Scheinfeld's," says the third. Benny slips and slides like an ice-skating giraffe until he's finally standing. Wiping his brow with the back of his hand, it's as if he's reached an island in a sea of slippery floor.

That's Shira's cue. While the nurses try to catch their breath from laughing, she sneaks unseen into Rose Morgenstern's room. And there's Esther! The girls are reunited!

Esther jumps from Rose's side and embraces Shira. "Your audition was wonderful, Shira! Congratulations."

Shira squeezes her hard. "I have so much to tell you."

To be next to her look-alike, her partner in crime, Esther feels a surge of relief.

"I need your help," they say at the same time.

"You, first." They try again but still speak over one another. They laugh.

"Esther." Rose's voice is weak, but serious. "You go first."

Esther, slowly, solemnly, says, "Shira, I think you and I are cousins."

Shira isn't solemn at all. She squeals and grabs Esther back into a big hug. Her heart feels full to bursting, and she's not sure if the thumping is coming from her chest or Esther's. Do they share a heartbeat in their excitement now?

"Birthday twins first, and now cousins? Esther, what do you mean?"

Now Esther's words are flying while she races into her story. She explains the inscription on the cookbook, the photo on the rabbi's desk, the features she shares with Mel, breaking the frame, ripping the photograph, how Idylldale is big but not that big, and how Fanny might not have even told Mel that Esther existed! "I want him to come to the bat mitzvah."

Now Shira is solemn. "So, of course we invited him. He's my uncle. But he hasn't visited in ages, and the invitation just went to the last address we had. He moves around a lot; the last we knew he was selling cars. Papa said he might not even get it."

This stops Esther. She chews on her thumb.

"Papa hasn't scolded you about nervous habits yet?" Shira says, taking Esther's hand in her own. "Listen. Even though Uncle Coop isn't around much, he's kind and generous. He sends me a birthday card every year. Ooh, you should read them."

Esther remembers the first day she came to the rabbi's house with Benny, and a memory clangs into her head with new meaning. "Are those the cards tied with a ribbon in your closet? In a shoebox? I read a few of the early ones but they don't say much. I forgot all about them!"

"Oh, they get better," Shira says, with a wave of her hand. "I promise. Maybe you'll find something to explain why he left in the first place. Look, if he knew you existed, I'm sure he'd be here. We just have to figure out a way to tell him."

"But there's more."

"More than finding out who your father is?" Shira laughs at this wonderful adventure that just keeps getting wilder.

Esther nods. "*Your* father is concerned about the speech. And he should be. I haven't written it yet. I think . . . I don't want to do it alone, and I actually don't want to take your bat mitzvah away. It's your ceremony, even if I want my own. So . . ." She swallows. "What if we do it together? You can help me with the service—taking the Torah from the arc, and so forth. He thinks I—*you*—know how to do all that already."

Shira squeezes Esther's hand again. "Absolutely. Yes, to everything. Especially because I need you too." She shakes her head. "Get a load of this: Fanny owes a ton of money to this guy, Alexander Malaise. He's who owns the Heights, and he keeps raising the rent even though ticket sales are down. Look." Shira retrieves the telegram she intercepted.

As Esther reads it, Shira and Benny watch as her eyes grow as big as bobbins too. "After the performance on Thursday night—bulldozers are coming? What will Mama do for work?" Esther wants to tear up the telegram and stomp on it. "Where will we go?"

"Everyone's been hoping that if I, well *you*, win the thousand bucks, they'll have enough to pay their bills, but it sounds like this Malaise guy has had a parking lot in mind all along." Shira pauses. "I guess when you switch places with a girl, you get the good and the bad parts of her life. Now we're both in this mess."

"You're right about that." Esther shakes her head, worry settling in the pit of her stomach. "We didn't see this one coming, that's for sure."

"What if I mess up and lose the Heights for all of Idylldale? What if I only made it past the audition because a pipe burst on my head, and I kept going? What if that's different from being talented?" The confidence and joy Shira usually wears like an easy pair of pants has been replaced with the tightness of a twisted skirt. "I'll do whatever I can, but I'd rather do it *with you*. I think we'll be better together."

Esther switched places with Shira specifically because she didn't want to perform, but now the Heights, her home, is in danger. If she says no, she'd be abandoning her theater family and everything she loves. "Okay," she says. "I'll perform for you and for the Heights. You'll help with the bat mitzvah for me and your father."

"Remember, Esther, almost everyone watches the *Nicky Sanders Show*. Children. Fathers. Even uncles. And if you say something on live TV, Uncle Coop might hear you."

"Mel."

They squeeze each other's hands.

"Girls," Rose pipes up. "You do realize that for your plan to work, you'll need to come clean to those parents of yours?"

Esther nibbles at her thumb, and Shira crosses her arms.

"Listen. You've both done something wrong by switching places." The girls feel a moment of shame until they see a twinkle in her eyes. "Have you enjoyed it?"

"So much," Shira says without pause.

"I'm glad we switched," Esther says. "Not everything went the way I wanted, but I'm starting to get used to that too."

"Then perhaps the something wrong was actually the right thing to do," Rose says. "You can tell that rabbi of yours I said that. Just don't make it a habit."

The plan to find Esther's father and steal the show—and save the theater—starts tomorrow.

ACT III

CHAPTER TWENTY-FIVE

A FATHER, AN UNCLE, AND AN AUNT

EVERY DAY FOR THE last week, Shira's closet has been Esther's own, and even though Shira's shoes are a bit big, she's lined up the once-scattered pairs. The shoebox with the makeup gets pulled out every morning to hide her mole, but two boxes have remained in the closet—one with the too-small dance shoes and the other with the envelopes wrapped in red ribbon. Now they take center stage.

Rabbi Epstein is snoring in his room when Esther slips the red ribbon off the letters. She is as hopeful as the day is new, and with hands shaking in anticipation of finding out about the man who is probably her father, she opens each of the twelve cards—one for every birthday she and Shira shared.

As she promised, on Shira's sixth birthday the notes start to change.

Dear Kiddo,
Six years old! I'll bet you're reading this all by yourself
this year. After many years of selling encyclopedias,
Uncle Sam has me recruiting soldiers for the US
Government. Here's a dollar to buy a bond.
Love you,
Uncle Coop

Fanny always told her that her thirst for knowledge came from Mel selling encyclopedias! Uncle Coop and her own father have to be the same person. They just *have* to! Esther hugs the note to her chest.

She digs into the next letters with new longing. They each have a postmark from the same army base and an added postscript. For Shira's seventh birthday it says, *PS: Facts about your mother. Mona loved strawberry ice cream.* And then it hits her. If her father is Shira's uncle, then Mona would have been Esther's aunt. A sadness washes over her, and she wants to know more.

When Shira turned eight, Mel wrote, *PS: Mona was a great dancer.* Shira must have loved to learn that fact. At nine, Mel told Shira, *Mona named all the cows on our farm outside of Chicago. Her favorite was a Jersey with big, brown eyes and long lashes named Malka.* Esther imagines a younger version of the man from the rabbi's torn photograph milking brown cows.

When Shira turned ten, the envelopes were posted from Connecticut, one of them on stationery from the Fuller Brush Company. The postscript read, *Mona always dreamed of traveling to Holland to see the windmills when the tulips were in bloom.*

Esther giggles. No wonder there are so many windmills in Shira's house. Still from Connecticut, the eleventh birthday fact says, *Mona loved the Sabbath. Your father fell in love with her when he was an assistant rabbi at our temple in Chicago. Ask him about it.*

Esther realizes: If Mona is her aunt, then Rabbi Epstein is her uncle. She'll be able to continue her studies, ask him her questions, and even visit when Fanny is being difficult. They can celebrate holidays together! She's gained a father, an aunt, and an uncle in one afternoon. She raises her eyes to the heavens, takes a deep breath, and says, "Thank you."

She reads on. Last year's card, from an auto dealer's address, says, *Mona was a great mom. She took care of me after our parents died in a car accident when I was twelve—the age you are now.*

As she reads these bits and pieces about Mona and Mel's life, Esther has more questions than answers. She goes to the window and watches the western sky light up as the sun, rising behind her, stretches its beams across Idylldale from the center of town to the Heights to the textile mill. She sees the mist rise from the Idylldale River. She's happy about her newfound family. But right this moment, she misses her mother terribly.

Sitting at Shira's desk, in careful cursive, she copies the Chicago auto dealership address from Mel's last envelope on to a piece of paper. Here's hoping he's still there.

To: Melvin Cooper

Hudson Motor Showroom

Michigan Avenue

Chicago, IL

Dear Mel (stop) I'm Frances (Red Hot Fanny)

Rosenbaum's daughter (stop) I think you're my father

(stop) Shira and I to be bat mitzvahs this Saturday

(stop) Performing on Nicky Sanders Show Thursday

night 7 p.m. (stop) Come to Idylldale ASAP (stop)

She is careful to wipe the tears that surface before they drip on the ink. She chews on the pen top. She can't quite bring herself to write *Love*. Sincerely? Fondly?

Hopefully, Esther Rosenbaum

Then as Shira, Benny, and Esther discussed, she shakes out the piggy bank on Shira's dresser and counts enough for five cents per word. She leaves a note for Rabbi Epstein so he'll go to the hospital for Rose without worrying where she is. Finally, she makes her way to the Trolley Transfer Station to meet Benny and buy a telegram at Western Union.

Their plan is in motion.

CHAPTER TWENTY-SIX

A POTATO SACK BIMA

MORTY OPENS THE BACK door of the deli for Benny, and a small, stooped lady, with an oversize hat and sunglasses, enters from the alleyway too.

"I'm sorry, Miss," Morty says. "The back door is just for deliveries."

"Morty!" Esther says, taking off the disguise. "It's me."

"Ah! What do I know. I'm just the deli man, and it's not easy to tell who's who these days." Morty wipes his hands on his apron. He retrieves a salami hanging from the ceiling for the storefront.

Between two Frigidaire iceboxes, flour and sugar sacks huddle. Shira stands behind a tower of crates containing leafy and colorful produce.

"What do you think of our potato sack *bima*?" She extends her arm with the energy of a car salesman or a game show host. "Ready to show me what you've learned, Esther?" Shira settles against the shelves of pickled beets and pickled pickles that line the wall.

Esther takes a breath and tries not to giggle nervously. Up until now, only the rabbi has heard her chant her portion. When she and Shira first met, she bristled, defensive that she might not be Jewish enough. Here she is, a week later, with Shira's Torah portion memorized. Is she more Jewish than she was before? Shira has been studying theater for a week instead of focusing on her bat mitzvah. Is she less Jewish?

"C'mon. Put on your rabbi face." Shira waves her hand over her own face. Up: happy; down: serious.

"Shir," Esther giggles. "Studying Torah is joyful."

Hands on hips, Shira gives her a look. "Maybe for you. You can't tell me you didn't get the Rabbi Epstein hawk eyes when you ripped that picture."

Esther shivers. "Oh, I most certainly did. I had to write lines too."

"'To everything there is a time and purpose'?"

"Yes!"

The girls laugh and roll their eyes and shake their heads about Fanny and Rabbi Epstein, and it looks like the best of times. But this intimate understanding of someone else's parent is rare. They almost feel like sisters.

Finally, their conversation returns to the Torah portion.

"Wow! You've learned all that in a week!" Shira says. "All memorized? You're not reading?"

"Nope. I can follow along enough to fool the rabbi, but I don't know all the vowels."

They get down to business. Shira shows Esther how each Hebrew letter works to create the words she's saying. When they get to the vowels, Shira says, "There's a few different ways to write each one."

I'm sure you're familiar with doing homework. Isn't it surprising how much more fun it is doing it with a buddy than studying alone? That's what Shira and Esther feel— both of them—and they don't even need to say it out loud.

"Okay. You ready to learn to carry a Torah scroll?"

Foolishly, Esther pats her pockets. "Um . . . Sorry, I left mine at home."

"Look who's the comedian now," Shira says. She asks Benny for help, and he hands Esther two nine-pound blue-ribbon kosher beef bologna tubes for her to rest on her shoulder. If you think scroll and imagine a piece of paper, you'd be correct, *kinder*. But a whole Torah scroll is *five* books on a single piece of paper all rolled up, so those two tubes of bologna feel just about right.

"What if I drop them?"

"That's how you make meatballs," Benny jokes.

"Actually," Shira says, "if a Torah gets dropped, the whole congregation has to fast, so don't do that." She's right. Who wants to refuse food when they could be eating my knishes?

Next, the girls divvy up the service prayers and begin to practice, and Morty comes in just so he can hear them sing. What can I say? Their harmonies during "Oseh Shalom" are irresistible.

When the song is done, Esther opens a small notebook. "Okay. We need to write this speech." She taps her pencil on her lips. "The portion is all about honoring and obeying your parents." She writes, *Obey parents?*

Benny scoffs. "Because you both know all about that."

Shira whacks his shoulder.

"Focus," Esther directs. "The thing is, the Torah portion says to obey parents as one might obey God."

Shira shakes her head vigorously, "But they're not God. They're human."

"They make mistakes all the time," Benny chimes in.

"They disappear," Esther says.

"They die," Shira says. She shakes out her legs as if she could shake off her deepest loss and paces the small back room.

"This week at the theater has been the best week of my life. No books at all, which is . . . great. Why can't he just understand that I'm different from him?"

"Fanny doesn't even try to understand," Esther says. "She just dismisses my interest in Torah. I can't figure out if she thinks it's a phase I'll grow out of, or if she's worried I'll embrace it the rest of my life—and leave her?"

Their frustration hangs in the room like the meat on the ceiling, heavy and silent.

"I'm sure they mean well," Esther says softly. "Your father says parents know what's best for their children."

Shira rolls her eyes. "He'll know after the *Nicky Sanders Show*."

And, *kinder*, maybe it *will* take some time for the rabbi and Fanny to understand more: two girls, two gifts, two paths, one speech. Finished! You wanted to hear it now? Keep your shirt on; we'll get there.

CHAPTER TWENTY-SEVEN

A POTATO SACK TV CAMERA

ON WEDNESDAY, THERE'S ONE day left until the Nicky Sanders live television event. Esther wears her hat and sunglass disguise again. In town, she checks the Western Union telegram office, finds there's been no reply from Mel, and sneaks to the back room of the deli.

Fanny, Millie, Levi, and Joshua are windswept in a storm of seamstresses, musicians, and engineers the *Nicky Sanders Show* has sent to get the Heights shipshape for showtime.

Shira might as well be invisible as she darts in and out to get extra rain boots and a raincoat for Esther.

At the ticket booth, people are lined up, and everyone has something to say.

"They can shine the brass doors all they want. You can't make a silk purse out of a sow's ear."

"Nicky Sanders is so dreamy."

"About time this theater put on something other than Yiddish shows."

"They're finally joining the twentieth century."

"Whaddya mean? The Yiddish theater *is* Idylldale."

In Morty's back room, Benny and Esther are using the stacked potato sacks as a stand-in for the TV camera. Benny plays the director and camera operator. "And action!"

"Wait," Shira says. "I want us to sing the chorus in Yiddish."

"Cut!" shouts Benny. "You want us to rewrite the lyrics so close to the show?"

"Why?" Esther asks.

"Well, you know I've loved being on the stage, but I've also loved watching the Yiddish troupe perform *Beauty and the Shlemiel*. It's so funny! And each night in the show, Fanny sings 'Abi Gezunt'—'As Long as You're Well.' It swings here at the theater and lulls me to sleep at your apartment. Yiddish is part of what makes the Heights—the Heights."

Esther smiles big. "Well, when you put it that way . . . Let's do it! Let's bring a little Yiddish to our TV audience."

"Yeah!" Benny encourages.

"So, yes? But I'll need your help to translate 'take good care of yourself, you belong to me.'"

"Well if we make it fit the music, it would be '*hit zikh, hit zikh gor gut, du geherst tsu mir.*' Does that sound good?"

"It sounds great!" Shira says. She practices the new pronunciation with Esther helping on each syllable.

Together, they practice "Button Up Your Overcoat" with the new chorus. They rework the choreography to include Esther, and they add in some back-and-forth to show Shira's comic timing. And even though I'm just the deli man, I know something fabulous when I see it.

With the sun sinking in the west, the rabbi sitting at Rose's hospital bedside, the tickets sold out, and the theater more abuzz than ever, Esther, Shira, Benny, and

Morty use a piece of chalk to draw a map of Idylldale on the floor of the storage room. With a potato as a stand-in for each of the adults in their lives, they plot their secret strategy for show night. Tomorrow, they'll meet back at the deli at 4:30 p.m.—a half an hour before call time.

If their plan doesn't work, the bulldozers are coming.

Thursday morning, zippy cars, clunky trucks, and loud voices at the stage loading dock pull Shira to the window. "They're *here!*"

"Doesn't anyone respect a girl's beauty rest?" Fanny mumbles.

"Don't you want to see the television people, Mama?"

"Oh, they're no different than any other people," Fanny says, and covers her head with a pillow.

Shira gets dressed and runs out of the apartment building in time to see Levi rolling up the massive stage door. The parade of television equipment for the *Nicky Sanders Show* begins.

First come three large cameras, then heavy stepladders with rolling wheels, then massive lights and still more lights, then miles and miles of cables and cords, then microphones and large black suitcases with who-knows-what inside.

When things get set up, Shira nudges Levi to introduce her to the director, Mr. Leonard, a thin man with tired eyes and a threadbare but comfortable-looking cardigan.

"Can I help, Mr. Leonard? I want to know everything about show business."

"Sure, little lady! We're setting up the sound system now, so first things first: We need your levels. Just stand over there under the boom and talk," he tells her, and points to a capsule-shaped microphone as big as her head suspended on the end of an extremely long pole. "Go ahead."

Shira pauses before she launches into the joke she told Rose. "A man walks into a tailor's," she says, "and the tailor gives him a suit. And the man says, 'But the left leg is too long.'" Just like in the hospital, it gets a laugh from the crew before she even finishes. She keeps the joke going until she gets a thumbs-up from the sound engineer in front of a board with dials and needles that jump when she speaks.

When Nicky Sanders comes in, she watches while he rehearses the monologue. She barely breathes through the whole thing.

Finally, Millie drags her away from the band rehearsal.

"Millie, is TV always so exciting?"

"One person's dream is another person's nightmare," she says. "Come on. The other acts should be here any minute."

"Already 4:15?"

Millie looks at her watch and nods.

Dressed in her costume, Shira runs upstairs to the stage door, down the alley, and into Morty's shop. "Where's Esther?" Morty shrugs.

It's a more complicated question than it sounds.

The rabbi is alone when Frank's shadow falls over his figure in the sanctuary of the synagogue. He stops rocking in prayer and looks up. "Yes?"

"Rabbi? Excuse me. There is a Western Union boy here with a telegram."

"Well, tell him to give it to you." He rocks again, eyes closed—an open prayer book in his hands.

Frank clears his throat. "I would have but, Rabbi, the sender is . . ."

The rabbi sighs. "Frank, who? Just tell me."

"He says it's from Shira."

Rabbi Epstein opens his eyes and looks up at the towering man. "*My* Shira?"

Frank just nods.

"Young man," he says, striding outside to the boy on the bicycle, giving him the look that turns Shira and Esther to Jell-O. "What is the meaning of this? A telegram from my own daughter?"

"I don't read the telegrams, sir. I only deliver them. This one says, 'For Rabbi Samuel Epstein, from Shira Epstein.' So if you're Rabbi Epstein, you know more about it than I do." Then, scared by his own impertinence, the telegram boy hops on his bicycle and kicks off without even asking for a tip.

"I don't believe it," says the rabbi, peering at the telegram. Sure enough, it's from Shira. He rips it open.

PERFORMING TONIGHT IN NICKY SANDERS'S SHOW—(STOP)—
7 P.M.—(STOP)—TICKET WAITING FOR YOU AT THE HEIGHTS—
(STOP)—KNOW YOU'RE DISAPPOINTED I DISOBEYED—(STOP)—
HAVE TO FOLLOW MY HEART—(STOP)
YOUR SHIRA

Rabbi Epstein, confused, thinks back to the night they watched the show together and Shira asked his permission to audition. He had clearly said no, and she's been doing nothing but diligently studying her Torah portion since then. How could she be in the show? In fact, he remembers the dinner with Shira reading the paper, saying her friend had been chosen for the show, the argument they had, the way she had stomped off. He heads into his office for his coat and is glad to find Frank still there, changing a light bulb.

"Frank? What's all this about Nicky Sanders coming to Idylldale?"

"*Nu?* He's the most famous person to visit Idylldale since Sophie Tucker. And . . . there was a plumbing emergency during the auditions that I had to fix."

"Do you know how many children were chosen?" he asks.

"Yes, five. I'm taking my wife to see it this evening."

"You're not going to believe this, but Shira has sent me a telegram saying that she is in the show!"

"Well." The rabbi is shocked at how unsurprised Frank sounds. "The girl has been acting odd."

"What do you mean, *the girl*? Shira?"

Frank looks down at his feet, which are a long way away from his head, and back to Rabbi Epstein. "Rabbi, if I may speak plainly."

"Please," Rabbi Epstein says, motioning with his hands.

"The girl doesn't walk like Shira. She doesn't tell jokes like Shira. And now she wants to read and study? That's not our Shira."

If he is honest with himself, the rabbi knows that something has been amiss too. He never needs to remind her to practice her portion. She chants it at all hours of the day and night. The way Shira, or . . . whoever she is, held Rose's hand when they visited? Frank is right, and the rabbi is all agog.

He is agog because Frank just told him that his daughter isn't his daughter. But this we already knew.

Gripping the telegram tightly, he rushes to the trolley, but he's stopped by Benny. "Rabbi Epstein, your cab is waiting."

"*My* cab?"

"Shira said you'd need one." Benny opens the door to the car idling next to him, and the rabbi gets in, dazed. "Enjoy the show!" Benny slaps the roof of the taxi, and they're off.

As they drive, Rabbi Epstein thinks back, wondering when he first felt things were off with his daughter. Or maybe he should say *the girl*. Who is she? When did she arrive? He can't believe his own memory.

Esther, in the overcoat and rain boots from Millie's fabulous costume closet, stands outside the door of the Heights and takes a deep breath. *Honesty*, she tells herself when Rabbi Epstein emerges from the cab. She approaches.

"Good evening, Rabbi, I'm Esther Rosenbaum. Shira isn't here yet, but I wanted a moment to explain why I've been studying with you the past two weeks."

"I thought Esther was Shira's friend. The one with the mother?" Rabbi Epstein says, bewildered. He still can't believe his mistake. "The one who auditioned for Nicky Sanders?"

"No, *that* was Shira."

Rabbi Epstein is perplexed. He reads the telegram in his hand again as if it will tell him something new, then looks at the girl in front of him. "What have you done with my daughter this whole time?"

"Me? Nothing. She's been here at the Heights with my mother, safe and sound and happy."

"So, she's been fed?"

Even in the stress of the situation, Esther can't help but cough out a laugh. "Yes, she's had plenty to eat. Rabbi, I'm so sorry. I didn't want to lie. Remember, I did tell you the truth right away! I'm a performer's child who wants to be a bat mitzvah."

"The night with the chicken and the potatoes? I thought you—Shira—was feverish. Ill! You mean . . ."

Esther ducks her head. "That was me. I've wanted to work with you for a long time. My mother . . . she doesn't understand why I want to read Torah and study."

He looks from Esther to Shira's telegram and back again. *Have to follow my heart.*

"Shira misses you," Esther adds, seeing the pain on his face. "But . . . she has a wonderful voice and she dances like a dream. She needs the stage. And really, the stage needs her."

He cannot believe that for almost two weeks he has been living with—and loving—an imposter. How is this possible? What would his wife, Mona, God rest her soul, say if she were alive today? What would she say if she knew he couldn't recognize their own daughter?

I'll tell you what she'd say, *mayne kinder.* She'd say, *Husband. You didn't expect an imposter, so you didn't see an imposter.*

You cared for this girl as if she were your own when she needed
help and love. You taught her Torah when she looked for learn-
ing. Do not be angry at her, and be gentle with Shirala. She loves
you so.

"But, Esther . . . who *are* you? How do you look so much like my daughter?"

"This is the real mystery . . . I think I'm your niece?"

Rabbi Epstein is a little dizzy. "So Mel is . . ."

"My father, I think? That's why I was looking at the photograph in your office. I'm so sorry I ripped it."

"But who's your mother?"

"That one I know. Frances Rosenbaum is my mother."

"The actress?" he asks, pointing at the marquee above him. "She named you Esther," he says, his mind swirling. "'That means 'a queen who led her people.' She must see a bright future for you," he says.

"Well, yes. But our ideas of my future aren't the same." Esther had been starving for a teacher, and Rabbi Epstein nourished her heart and mind. "With your help, I'm following my heart. Thank you."

"A teacher is only as good as their student. Esther, you are a wonderful student. I may have been wrong about disobeying your mother to study, but nonetheless: I was honored to have you on the *bima* with me."

She inches closer to Rabbi Epstein with open arms. She hugs him, and he hugs her back.

Taxi doors slam.

Ushers take tickets.

Trolley bells clang.

"Esther? Where is Shira now? I'd like to see her."

"Oh dear. We're late!" She pats the rabbi's arm. "Follow me."

Their plan is working.

CHAPTER TWENTY-EIGHT

THE NICKY SANDERS SHOW

"KEEP THAT DOG QUIET when we're live!" shouts Mr. Leonard, as Violet's dancing dog barks backstage. "Do we have some meat or something?"

"I can get some!" Shira bolts toward the stage door. Esther wasn't at Morty's at 4:30, and Shira has been checking the alleyway every chance she gets. Now, an hour later and thirty minutes till showtime, the rabbi should be taking his seat in the front row.

She scans the alley, rushes past Saul's, and slides into Morty's out of breath. "Is she here?"

Morty shakes his head and wipes his hands on his apron, more from nerves than anything sticky. They press their foreheads to the window.

"Do you think she's okay?"

"Of course I think she's okay! But what do I know, I'm just . . ."

"The deli man," they finish together.

A trolley car on Main Street stops and pulls away. Two more taxis go by. None seem to deposit the rabbi. "Do you think my father kept her from coming?"

Morty shrugs. "It's possible."

"Is he going to come take me home?"

"It's possible."

"He's going to kill me."

"Nah, that one's not possible." Morty pushes away from the window and crooks his finger under her chin. "Then he'd have to find someone else to make knishes."

"Oh, I almost forgot!" Shira remembers her original mission. "Can I have a slice of salami for the dog act?"

"A dog act? *Feh*. You and Esther are going to win this thing."

"From your mouth to God's ears." The voice freezes Shira to the spot.

"Papa?" She turns. Her father is as out of place among the deli cases as I would be at a conference of rabbis. Next to him, finally, is Esther, tugging his hand to pull him into the store.

"Please don't be angry, Papa," Shira says.

"I'm a little angry about the lying. I was *a lot* worried when I got your telegram." He reaches out and cups her cheek—then smears the mole-colored makeup on her neck. The rabbi smiles, but it's tinged with regret. "Mostly, though, I am sad. Sad that I didn't know. Sad that I wasn't the kind of father you could trust with your dreams."

He clasps her to his chest. He smells like aftershave and a little like the hospital. Squeezing her eyes shut, Shira pictures his orderly closet, the windmills, his bliss when she makes his favorite dinner. "Oh, Papa, I'm sorry." Her words muffle in his shirt. "But sometimes, it's so hard for me to be what you want . . ."

"Shira, I just want you to be who you are."

She shakes her head. "No."

Mayne kinder, do remember how Esther made up a story about her father because she didn't know the truth? Shira has one too. A story that she told herself over and over again until she assumed it was true.

She squeezes tighter so she can say what's on her mind, so he can't release her, so he can't see her worry. "When I want to be funny, to stand out . . . you want a perfect Rabbi's Daughter, and . . . you want Mama." Her voice hitches in her throat. "I think . . . I know it's my fault she's gone."

"Shira, no."

"It's true, and I just . . ." She burrows deeper into his chest. "I wonder if it would have been better if I died instead of Mama." Esther and Morty gasp. In Shira's hands, the salami is misshapen and squished from her truth.

The rabbi gets down on his knees. He wipes at the tears that flood her eyes and drip down her cheeks. "Oh, my sweet Shira. Death is so hard for any of us to understand. But hear me." He takes her face in his hands. "I know this for sure: You are not at fault for your mother's passing, and I'm grateful every day for you. You are the perfect Rabbi's Daughter because I am a rabbi, and you are my daughter. That is all that matters."

"You mean it?"

"Of course! I love all of you. The way you think." He kisses her *keppie*. "The way you care for others." He touches her heart with his finger. "I especially love your joke about the tailor." At that, the rabbi pops up and does the same silly walk that Shira showed Rose in her hospital room. He picks her up, spins her with ease, and puts her down. "Shira. You are the joy of my life. Nothing will change that."

She laughs and wipes the wetness from his cheeks.

"I'm sorry to interrupt, Rabbi," Esther says. "But we need to go before Miss Hayes worries. And you and Morty have to get seats!" She hands them their tickets and pulls Shira away from the man who loves them both.

Shira leans into Esther's shoulder as they cross the street. "I can't believe that happened."

"He loves you, Shir. And love and honesty go hand in hand."

"How'd you get so smart?"

"I had a good teacher." Esther gives her a kiss on the cheek. "We can do this?"

"We can definitely do this!"

"For the Heights?"

"For the Heights!"

Back in the theater, Miss Hayes flits from makeup, where Nicky Sanders is surrounded by a cloud of powder, to Mr. Blum, who is rehearsing with his band, to Fanny and Millie, who are choosing and rechoosing the wardrobe for the evening, to Miss Scheinfeld, who is reading and rereading her short script. Mr. Leonard holds his hands up square, thumbs together, framing shot after shot. "Live, people. This one is live!" he keeps saying.

Levi pops his head into the theater and calls out, "I'm opening the house in ten."

"Thirty minutes to air, people," the director says.

Shira, having left Esther behind the back curtain, flattens herself against the stage wing wall when a *shtarker* moving a set trundles by.

"Bull! Bring that over here," Mr. Leonard calls.

"I don't mean to push you out of the way, kid, but Miss Hayes wants all the children in the chairs set up stage right,"

Bull tells her. He lifts a seven-foot-tall Nibbles potato chip bag as if it were a regular one.

Everything about him, from his deep rumbly voice to his strength to his nickname, reminds her of the bulldozers that Mr. Malaise will be sending the next day unless she and Esther can win the money to save the Heights.

On the wall, the stage manager has posted the run of the show.

Opening and Credits . . . Orchestra
Scheinfeld's Advertisement . . . Miss Rosenbaum & Miss Scheinfeld
Nibbles Advertisement . . . Mr. Sanders
Monologue . . . Mr. Sanders

CHILDREN'S TALENT SHOW
(1) Song & Dog . . . Violet
(2) Poetry Recitation . . . Gertie
(3) Violin . . . Jack
(4) Juggling . . . David
(5) Song & Dance . . . Esther
Duet . . . Miss Rosenbaum & Mr. Sanders

AWARDS
Closing . . . Full Cast

She peeks through the curtain to find her father and Morty in the audience. Their heads are together as they review the playbill. Her papa points at something and they laugh, but feeling her gaze, he glances in her direction, catches her eye, and puts both hands on his heart.

She told him everything and he understood.

Holy casserole! Following her heart never felt so good.

CHAPTER TWENTY-NINE
LIVE

ESTHER FEELS THE TELEVISION lights, hot as the sun, heat up the entire backstage. They seem to illuminate the obstacles she and Shira are up against: She'll have to stay hidden until it's their turn to go on, and then they have to do the number better than they've ever done it before. Promptly at six o'clock, the orchestra begins the opening credit music, and Esther watches Fanny roll her shoulders back and pinch her cheeks. Esther does the same.

Offstage, Shira can't sit still. Her heart is like a metronome that gets set faster and faster; she is *shvitzing* but shivering at the same time. It's the first time she can remember feeling impatient through any music at all, but finally, the orchestra is done with their show overture.

After Fanny and Miss Scheinfeld perform an advertisement for the resort and hotel, and Nicky Sanders sings the Nibbles potato chip jingle, he delivers his monologue. And guess what? He tells the joke about the tailor and the man with the ill-fitting suit. Shira's favorite! She hopes Rose is watching at the hospital and that it makes her papa laugh. Somehow, she is performing on the same stage as Nicky Sanders . . . Nicky Sanders!

And while she wants to savor every moment of this night, she's also eager to perform. Her stomach does a little skip when she thinks about her father in the front row beyond the lights. She glances back at the curtain, and Esther, still hiding, gives her a thumbs-up.

Violet and her dog finish, then Gertie is done with her poem. As soon as they hear the end of Jack's violin piece, Shira takes her place in the stage right wing. Thankfully, Miss Hayes is rapt, watching David juggling—because from offstage, David's father has thrown in an unexpected fifth ball. For a moment, David juggles steadily, but, just as the audience starts to applaud, he drops all the balls. They groan.

As the balls skitters across the stage, Esther sneaks up behind Shira with fresh stage makeup, and they squeeze. "For the Heights?"

"For the Heights."

David is bowing, the crowd erupting into sympathetic applause, and Nicky Sanders claps as he comes onstage. "Well, David, that was fantastic for someone who's seven years old. How long have you been juggling?"

"Since I was little," David says, and the audience laughs.

Miss Hayes laughs too— until she turns to see two identical girls in overcoats and rain boots. She stutters and stammers but there's nothing she can do, because Nicky Sanders is saying, "And now, we have a girl who is no stranger to this theater, the daughter of the lovely Fanny Rosenbaum, Esther Rosenbaum!"

"That's me," calls the real Esther.

"It'll be great, Miss Hayes," whispers Shira.

Miss Hayes is all agog.

The introduction starts. Shira dances onto the stage. She stops, turns to the wing, and makes a huge *come on* wave of her arm. And now, on comes Esther. Let the jazz hands wave!

Mayne kinder, you've seen this dance move before, yes? No! Oh, it's very simple; try it with me now. Hands at your side, spread your fingers wide, and shimmy your hands. Very good! It looks great when a group does it together. Add in a jazz box step, and you've got something. You don't know the box step? *Oy*, I don't have time to teach you that.

When two girls go on the stage instead of one, the grown-ups in the wings are stunned.

As soon as her real daughter is next to the imposter, Fanny sees the scheme clearly. Like the rabbi, Fanny sinks her head into her hands, but while the rabbi felt inadequate, Red Hot Fanny just laughs. She's been hoodwinked. Duped! Deceived by her own daughter! Who is this sweet girl who fell into her life and into her love? The girl who has been sharing her bed and rehearsing so diligently?

"I'm Shira! Thank you all for coming out tonight to the historic Heights theater," Shira says with a perfectly synced kick ball change.

"I'm Esther! This building belongs to a man named Alexander Malaise, who is sending bulldozers tomorrow to turn it into a parking lot," Esther says, and they both spin.

An uncomfortable laughter fills the room.

"Sadly, that's not a joke," says Shira with a shuffle stomp.

Fanny feels her chin drop, and she reaches for the closest wall to steady herself. The band stumbles and stops. The girls don't. This is live TV; the show must go on!

Inspired, the band continues.

"Ladies and gentlemen, you can save the Heights!" Esther calls.

"Here in the theater or watching at home, dig deep into your pockets and purses to save Idylldale's Yiddish theater," Shira continues, and then both girls chorus, "On your way out, donate!"

They spin and extend an open hand to the back of the theater. The people in the audience turn their heads to see Benny and Morty—and Saul!—standing at the doors with pickle jars from the delis. Even the rivals have come together to save the theater!

"And now," says Esther, "this number goes out to her uncle, my father, Melvin Cooper! We'll see you at our bat mitzvah on Saturday."

And together they say, "A five, six, seven, eight!"

Fanny listens to this speech from her spot in the wings. All this time she was trying to protect her daughter from the hard truths of life, but these girls knew more than she did.

And the performer in Fanny can't help but notice: The new girl and Esther are perfect together. They sing beautifully. They do their comic dance. The act is better with the two of them. They even include Yiddish. "*Du geherst tsu mir,*" you belong to me, they sing. She's overcome with the love she feels for Esther and her new niece—body and soul.

So, Mel must have a sister or brother living in Idylldale, she thinks. *That's probably what brought him to Idylldale in the first place. Is that where Esther has been? Has she been with Mel himself? And he's coming to a bat mitzvah?*

We know Esther has been with Rabbi Epstein. We know Shira's mother, Mona, died on the day she brought her beautiful Shira into the world in a hospital room down the hall from Fanny's hospital room. And we know Mel is—

Well, *mayne kinder*, that's a good question. What do we know about Mel?

CHAPTER THIRTY

MELVIN COOPER

ENCYCLOPEDIAS, MILITARY RECRUITMENT, FULLER brushes, and now cars—selling is second nature to Melvin Cooper. He doesn't have to work hard to do it well, so he has plenty of time to consider what he'll tell his niece, Shira, about her mother on her annual birthday card. This one will be her thirteenth.

It is almost closing at the auto dealership on Thursday, with two days to go before Shira's birthday, when he writes, *PS: Mona made the best knishes.* He inserts thirty-six dollars (double *chai*) into the card when the Western Union delivery boy shows up on his bicycle. "Telegram for Melvin Cooper! Is there a Melvin Cooper here?"

Mel raises his hand.

"The address wasn't complete," says the delivery boy. "I musta been up and down Automobile Row a hundred times in the last two days."

I never get telegrams! Mel thinks. "Thanks for the effort," he says, handing the boy a quarter for a tip.

He reads the telegram once.

He reads it twice.

He checks his watch and runs into the break room where Joe, his manager, is watching a football game. He changes the channels until he hears, "Live from Idylldale, from the historic Heights theater . . . It's the *Nickyyyy Sanders Show.*"

Watching the television, Mel is all agog. There is the stage where he first fell in love with Fanny Rosenbaum, body and soul.

A heart is a gushy thing with right and left ventricles and atriums—four parts all together. There's nothing in a heart that can break like picture frame glass or rip like a photo, but Idylldale had tried its best.

When Fanny Rosenbaum said she was going on tour with that no-good showman, Nicky Sanders, and sent Mel away, that was the first time Idylldale broke his heart. It broke again when he came back to return to Idylldale for his niece's birth and saw Fanny's name still on the marquee of the Heights. That's when he knew Fanny hadn't left at all. Since then, he'd assumed she just told that story because she wanted him gone. And when his sister, Mona, passed away after the birth of his niece, Shira, it was one heartbreak too many. He left and never came back to Idylldale.

He closes his eyes, remembering back and back and back some more to the way the spotlight at the Heights made Fanny Rosenbaum's long red hair shimmer.

And then, as beautiful as that day thirteen years ago, Fanny Rosenbaum is singing. Even though she is in black and white, Mel sees her in full color. She has twisted and piled her red hair on her head, and her eyebrows arch over green eyes. Those are the same high cheekbones and soft skin. He remembers her scent—gardenias. Mel is *farblunget*—another fabulous Yiddish word that sounds like what it describes—mixed up, unsure of where to turn next.

He is transfixed by that no-good showman's monologue and David's juggling accident. He watches the band falter and then stop entirely. The two girls onstage seem to have gone off script. What's happening?

Mayne kinder, those are our two girls, of course, Shira and Esther. They say the Heights is in trouble, bulldozers are on the way. He hears his name! They say they are his daughter and his niece!

Now who's bulldozed?

"Did they just dedicate the song to you?" Joe says. "I didn't know you had a kid."

Like cables clipped to a car battery, a current has restarted Mel's broken heart. "Neither did I!" His voice rises in a frenzy. A wave of guilt crashes over him, and he slumps. "Oh, what she must think of me. I have to leave." He takes Joe by the shoulders. "I have to leave now."

"Mel? You all right, man?" Joe shrugs off his hands. "You can't just leave. These cars won't sell themselves."

Mel grips the telegram and heads for the door. He's not *farblunget* anymore. He has new direction. "Body and soul," he mumbles. "Body and soul."

CHAPTER THIRTY-ONE

A SURPRISE

AS SOON AS FANNY finishes her final duet with Nicky Sanders, she grabs Shira and Esther and pulls them into her dressing room. Back and forth she alternates between clutching them close and holding them at a distance to look between the two faces. "You pests. You are both *awful.* What were you thinking, Esther? Shira, I presume?" She can't stop kissing either of them.

"I missed you, Mama," says Esther, ever so sweetly.

"And where, pray tell, have you been missing me *from?*"

"From Shira's house with her father, Rabbi Epstein."

"Rabbi Epstein," Fanny breathes. "Did he have something to do with this?"

"No!" the girls refute in unison.

"Then you made your dream come true, with no help from me. If that isn't the most Esther you've ever been!" She turns to Shira. "Does your father know where you are, young lady?"

"We told him tonight. He's in the audience."

"But, Mama?" Esther stops her mother's urgency with a hand on her arm. "What about the act? How was it?"

"Esther." Fanny drops to her knees. "You looked like you were having fun, finally! It's the hope I had for you your whole life. And Shira, so talented, you've been working hard to build your craft. The two of you together? It was better than . . . a tower of Morty's knishes." She kisses each of them again. "Maybe too much on the jazz hands but . . ."

"Ma!" Esther laughs.

"What? I'm joking. Come." Just then, they hear Nicky from the stage above them. "Well, ladies and gentlemen, this has been quite a night."

Running to the wings, they see Nicky in the spotlight. "Everyone was just wonderful tonight, weren't they, folks?" The crowd roars.

"Like a tower of knishes," Fanny stage-whispers, and the three of them hold in giggles with their palms.

"Now, as I'm sure I don't have to remind you, this is a contest." The crowd hushes in anticipation. "So, it's time to give away some prizes. In third place, winning a month's supply of Nibbles potato chips . . ."

The girls look at each other and shrug. A month's worth of potato chips sounds tasty, but they have other plans.

"David, the not-perfect-but-always-persistent juggler!" Nicky sweeps his arm toward stage right, and David waves to the audience, grabbing a bag of potato chips and a gold card from Nicky.

He claps his hands and punches the sky. "That's the prize I wanted!"

"Stand right here, David. All right. In second place, winning a one-week stay at Scheinfeld's Resort and Cottages . . ."

Fanny wrinkles her nose, and Shira and Esther shake their heads. For them, only one prize matters.

"Violet and her fabulous four-legged friend, Poochie!"

It's first place or nothing now. Fanny, Shira, and Esther share a wide-eyed stare. This, *this* is what they hoped and worked for.

Poochie trots onstage balanced and bouncing on his hind legs. Violet takes her gold card. "Does Scheinfeld's allow dogs?" she simpers. The girls watch the camera pan to Miss Scheinfeld who nods delightedly, then the camera is back on Poochie, who does a backflip!

(Perhaps the real performer in that team was Poochie!)

"And now for our final prize. The first prize winner will receive one thousand dollars and perform with me, Nicky Sanders, comedy genius and author of the book, *Keep 'Em Laughing* (on sale now right here in the lobby!), with this very show, in a five-city tour to be broadcast on television around the nation. And that winner is . . ."

The drummer starts a roll that *rat-a-tat-tat*s through a silent theater. How expectant is the theater? As expectant as you when rugelach is cooling on the rack. You want to taste the freshly baked pastry, but you know it will burn your mouth! Esther, Fanny, and Shira make a ring with their hands and close their eyes. They imagine their names perched on Nicky Sanders's tongue. Shira and Esther. Shira and Esther. Shira and Esther. The drumroll is never-ending.

Mayne kinder, what if they win? Will Rabbi Epstein even allow Shira to go on a five-city tour to perform? And what about Esther? She didn't want a life in showbiz to begin with. Still, even though a win will raise challenges, they've figured out harder problems!

Except Nicky doesn't say Esther Rosenbaum or Shira Epstein. Nicky says . . .

"Jack Kaminsky!"

Have you ever jumped into a pool while your friends cheer? When you're in the air, the cheering is the loudest thing in your ears. But once you're submerged, the sound is filtered and fuzzy. For Esther and Shira, the applause and their feelings are just as cloudy.

To be honest, they hadn't thought about *what if* they lost. Now they worry that they haven't done enough to save the theater. They wonder about the donations Benny, Morty, and Saul are counting. And between you and me, they are thinking that on a scale of one to five knishes, that neither Jack's, nor David's, nor even Poochie's performance should have earned as many knishes as their own.

"We lost," Shira says. "After all that work. All that practice. How?"

"Not even the potato chips?" Esther says.

Onstage, Nicky Sanders is still talking. He has a new gold card in his hand. "So let's bring them onstage," he says. "Esther and Shira, come on out!"

"What?" Shira asks.

"Get out there," hisses Fanny, herding them onto the stage. "And *smile!*"

Esther and Shira hold hands and trot out and wave. What else to do?

"Ladies." Nicky bends a little to look the girls in the eyes. "You put on quite a show tonight. Our judges weren't sure what to do." He stands and addresses the main camera. "To remind you all, the rules state that no group acts would be allowed in this talent contest."

The girls stay still. A technicality? They lost on a technicality?

"But here's the thing. You had your community in mind when you broke the rules, and we just can't overlook your selfless act to save this historic building—and your outstanding performance, of course. Therefore, the *Nicky Sanders Show* will donate five hundred dollars to your efforts to save the Heights." The audience gasps.

"Five hundred dollars!" Esther says.

"Yes! But that's not all!"

The audience gasps again.

"The Nibbles Potato Chip Company also wants to honor the importance of this community theater by donating . . . another five hundred dollars!"

One thousand dollars? That's more dollars than Esther or Shira or any of their families have ever owned at one time. It's the same amount of money they would have been given if they had won the contest!

Shira speaks first. "Holy casserole!" What else to say?

"Mr. Sanders, and Mrs. um . . . Nibbles Potato Chips," Esther says, her voice breaking, "we are ever so grateful for your donations. Idylldale just isn't Idylldale without the Heights."

"Yes, thanks a ton," Shira says. "You're even better in person than on TV!"

Nicky knew that giving away money was good for the show, but now, he loses his celebrity composure and blushes at his own generosity. "Aw, it was nothing."

"Well, it was *everything* to us, and . . . Mr. Sanders?" Shira bats her eyes at the camera and nudges closer to Nicky Sanders.

"Yes?"

"Can I give you a kiss?"

Well, at that, the audience loses *its* composure. The crowd goes wild when Nicky Sanders offers his cheek and Shira gives him a big! old! smooch!

In the front row, Rabbi Epstein's face is in his palms.

The Heights fills with hoots and hollers, chants and cheering. After the final song, the applause, the hugging, and a few tears are done, Mr. Leonard calls, "That's a wrap!" Esther's sure the building itself is taking a bow.

CHAPTER THIRTY-TWO

YOU BELONG TO ME TOO

AS THE AUDIENCE LEAVES, Shira catches bits of conversations from backstage.

"Haven't been here in years."

"The place looks great."

"I hear they're going to bring in more movies."

"I'd come back for that."

"I hope I was on television! What a thrill!"

"Great show, Fanny." Nicky Sanders appears and smoothly slips his arm around Fanny's waist. "I asked you once thirteen years ago, and I'm not too proud to ask you again. What do you think about going on tour with me? We could use your voice and you could use a national stage."

Fanny doesn't even pause. "No, thanks, doll." She steps out of his grasp. "You changed your mind last time because this one was in my belly." She pats Esther's cheek. "For her sake, and for my new niece, I'm staying put."

"All right, all right," he chuckles. "Just promise, if you come to the Big Apple—any of you—you'll look me up."

Levi said Nicky Sanders was selfish, and Mel called him "a no-good showman," but now, he's leaving Idylldale as a knight in shining armor. And with Miss Hayes and Mr. Blum nipping at his heels, in a flurry of flash bulbs and signed photos, Nicky Sanders, the most famous visitor Idylldale's seen since Sophie Tucker, exits stage left.

And now for tonight's finale. Shira, Esther, Fanny, and Rabbi Epstein find a quiet place in the lobby and meet each other for the first time—as one family joined by two cousins.

"What you two did for the theater tonight? It was a little *meshuge*." Fanny takes a breath, hands on her chest, and her eyes settle on Esther. She may be a dramatic lady all the time, but once in a while, those emotions can't be faked. "It means the world to me."

"Miss Rosenbaum, have you ever thought about getting the theater designated as a historic landmark?" wonders the rabbi. "Or, what if there was an Idylldale orchestra?" His eyes are as bright as they are when he's officiating at a wedding. "I imagine *many* members of my congregation would pay for that. Oh, and maybe——"

Fanny's eyes start to shine, and with a gentle hand on his arm she says, "I'm so glad we're to be family."

"Me too!" the girls say at the same time.

But the mood changes when Rabbi Epstein pulls out the telegram Shira sent. "You followed your heart tonight?"

"I did," Shira said.

"And you've been following your heart with the rabbi?" Fanny asks.

"That's right," says Esther. "Over the last two weeks, I've studied my Torah. Shira and I have practiced together. Now I want to join Shira on the *bima* Saturday morning."

In the past, Esther's desire to study Torah made Fanny bristle. Fanny finds God in the light of the spotlight and a perfectly played scene, not in the sanctuary of a synagogue. She's always hoped that Esther would feel the same way. And Esther seemed to enjoy performing just now. Fanny had gotten her hopes up that maybe tonight would be the beginning of the mother-daughter act she's always dreamed of.

But if Essie is still committed to Torah learning, then what if she begins to look down on Fanny from that highest house on the hill? What if Esther sees Fanny as . . . *not enough?*

The silence between them swells and fills with the calls and shouts of the television roadies' goodbyes, congratulations, and see-you-soons.

But Shira, always knowing how to smooth someone's bristle, says, "*Got hot zikh bashafn a velt mit kleyne veltlekh.*" This is what she said when Esther was unsure at their first meeting, and she says it now, in a quiet voice that slices the silence. *God created for himself a world with many little worlds.*

Fanny hears Shira, and hears her *well.* Fanny wishes she could call a take-five to script this moment. Perhaps then she could write a monologue that captures the way she feels watching her daughter grow from girl to young woman. Her pride in Esther's persistence, her surprise that Esther took such a risk to follow her dreams. But the show must go on. So now, she simply holds Esther's cheeks in her hands. "Essie, you are not me. Your joy is different from my joy. And anyway, you've given this stage enough tonight. On to the *bima!*"

"Mama!" Esther throws her arms around her mother's waist and her breath catches: gardenia. "Thank you!"

"All right, all right. But don't think I'm making it a habit to wake up for services *every* Saturday morning," she says, rolling her eyes dramatically, and they all laugh.

While the spirit of yes is in the room, Shira speaks up. "Father, I need—"

But the rabbi stops her with an upturned palm. His face is hard. "Esther talked to me about the importance of the theater. While sometimes it's improper," he softens, "she showed me that the theater can bring joy to the disaffected." Shira feels hope spiral up her chest like ivy, unbidden and insistent. "I see now that you were meant to spread that joy. Who am I to put out the light God kindled?" He takes a deep breath. "And so. Miss Rosenbaum, do you know a good piano teacher? Maybe a theater troupe with shows appropriate for children?"

Shira throws her arms around the rabbi, who plants a kiss on his daughter's forehead. "*Du geherst tsu mir*, Shirala."

"You belong to me too, Papa," Shira says but she isn't done celebrating. She runs to Esther; they embrace and jump up and down. Finally, they shake their *tuchuses* like the monkey in the song to the north, south, east, and west.

Outside, the night air is sweet with possibility. Shira and Esther lead Fanny and Rabbi Epstein to Morty's deli, where Benny, Levi, Millie, Joshua, and Saul are already celebrating—knishes all around.

"Incredible," Rabbi Epstein says after his first bite. Then, his voice booms with pride. "Tomorrow, *both* girls will be on the *bima*. My niece." The rabbi puts an arm around Esther. "And my daughter." He wraps his other arm around Shira, and he holds them close.

"What a strange family we are," Fanny says, and everyone laughs.

It's about to get stranger.

CHAPTER THIRTY-THREE

A FINAL TELEGRAM

THE NEXT DAY, NICKY Sanders, Miss Hayes, Mr. Blum, and the rest of their crew pack up their rooms at Schein-feld's and call for the bellboy. Benny Bell has been waiting for this call.

"Good morning, Mr. Sanders," he says, gives his hat brim a tap, and smiles. But when Benny goes to pick up Nicky's suitcase, his sweet smile turns to a frown. Now he tries to move it with his back. It's as if the suitcase is filled with lead—he can't push or pull it. He skitters backward and forward. His body is a noodle, his eyes crossed with effort. Finally, he kicks one leg up and spins, the suitcase budges an inch, and he falls, exhausted, with his eyes crossed and a "Hoo, boy. That was heavy!"

Even I almost fell for that! Nicky can't help but crack up. "Kid, you got talent." He sticks out his hand and Benny shakes it. "Here's my card. Look me up if you ever come to New York."

"I'd like nothing more, sir!" When all the suitcases are loaded—Benny tries to be the right mix of show-off comedian and efficient bellhop—he gives the Nicky Sanders car two taps on top, and off they go.

Benny watches the line of cars wind down the hill into the city of Idylldale. He sees the beauty as Esther did so many days ago—the silver rope of river lassoing downtown on one side while the train tracks fence the other. It's a magical place.

Benny pats the business card in his breast pocket. "Nicky Sanders thinks I'm funny."

At the same time, in downtown Idylldale, Fanny, Esther, and Shira take their good luck, their hard-earned money, and all the donations to Western Union. Together they send one last telegram.

ALEXANDER MALAISE

MALAISE TOWERS

$1,500 TRANSFERRED TO YOUR ACCOUNTANT VIA WESTERN

UNION WIRE—(STOP)—THE HEIGHTS THEATER PAID IN

FULL—(STOP)—IDYLLDALE POLICE ALERTED—(STOP)—HALT

BULLDOZERS—(STOP)

FRANCES ROSENBAUM

ESTHER ROSENBAUM

SHIRA EPSTEIN

CHAPTER THIRTY-FOUR

MEL ARRIVES

LONG AFTER NICKY SANDERS leaves and the last trolley is tucked into the garage on Friday night, Mel rolls past the WELCOME TO IDYLLDALE sign and over the train tracks.

Back in the day, he would have stayed at the rooming house across from the mill, but a lot has changed in thirteen years. It seems impossible that thirteen years ago would feel like just yesterday, but time is different for children and grown-ups. One year, when you're thirteen, is one-thirteenth of your life. That's a lot! One year, when you're thirty-six, is only one thirty-sixth of your life. That's a tiny bit. So it seems that one day Mel is falling in love with Fanny, the young and beautiful actress, and the next, he's idling outside the theater knowing he has a thirteen-year-old daughter he's never met.

His daughter—that would take some time to get used to—sent him a telegram asking him to come. Esther: a new joy in his life.

And his niece. On the television, she looked so much like Mona, his darling sister. Shira: He can't wait to be reacquainted with her again.

And Fanny.

Mayne kinder, a lie by omission is still a lie. Withholding the existence of Mel's daughter cuts him like a serrated blade through a bagel—messy and sharp. How can he forgive her?

The marquee canopy in front of the Heights is as warm as he remembers, but the warmth can't alleviate his pain. Before a tear can fall, he drives on—past the darkened delis, the deserted library, and the empty Trolley Transfer Station.

In the center of town, a red light flashes—too-long, too-late, too-long, too-late. He wonders if he should turn around and leave. Not tonight.

There's a vacancy at Scheinfeld's Resort and Cottages.

Tonight, he'll wash off the road trip grime. Tomorrow, he'll decide what to do.

CHAPTER THIRTY-FIVE

A BAT MITZVAH

NOW WE'RE AT THE dessert part of the story. You know what that's like. You've eaten a huge feast and you think you're full until something sweet comes out of the oven. Suddenly, you have a little more room. Good thing too, because there's a smidge more to Esther and Shira's story.

Now, it's Saturday again. Who would have thought that so much could happen in just two weeks?

Benny, who has the day off from Scheinfeld's, runs through the brass doors of the Heights and down the repaired red carpet. He leaps to the stage, sending up a quick thank-you to the ceiling mural of clouds the color of salmon for bringing Nicky Sanders to Idylldale.

"Esther? Shira? Are you ready?" Before he can knock on Fanny's dressing room door, it opens wide. Fanny has twisted both girls' hair in curls on top of their heads. Millie made them outfits that fit them each just right. Esther is wearing a blue-green dress with a fitted waist and a ruffle around the V-neck and shoulders. She loves how the skirt floats when she turns. Shira has on a pantsuit of the same material and design. "You both look . . . really nice."

"Thanks, Benny," Esther says.

"What am I?" Fanny asks him. "Chopped liver?" She swoops past with a rustle of silk skirts.

"Hey." Esther points at Benny's chest. "You've got a little something." When he looks, she chucks his chin, and they all laugh.

Esther, Shira, Benny, Fanny, Millie, Levi, Joshua, his wife Minna and their two children, and even me, Morty, all board the eastbound trolley together.

"You nervous?" Shira asks Esther between trolley bell clangs.

"Maybe a little. But I've been waiting and wanting this for so long, right now I just have a huge sense of relief. It's like there are a bunch of helium balloons tied to my arms."

"And what about Mel?"

"Oh, that makes my stomach flip. Maybe he moved and never got the invitation or the telegram. Maybe he never heard us on TV. It was a long shot, so I doubt he'll be there. I'm sure less nervous to think he's not coming." Esther sighs and leans her head on Shira's shoulder, twining her fingers in her cousin's. "I just hope to meet him someday. At least now I know who he is."

Rabbi Epstein welcomes the group at the synagogue, grasping Fanny's hand in gratitude. His love for Esther and Shira makes him light on his feet as he ushers them away to get ready for the ceremony.

Mayne kinder, you've been to a bat mitzvah, yes? Oh, you haven't?! So much *naches*, joy and pride. A child becomes an adult in the eyes of the community—two children, in this case! The congregation stands, the congregation sits. They sing when they're told to sing, they read when they're told to read, and sometimes everyone is quiet.

On the *bima*, there are prayers for candles and prayers for wine. Rabbi Epstein calls Levi to say a prayer that honors the gift of Torah. *Barukh atah Adonai, notein hatorah.* Finally, the girls and Rabbi Epstein turn to the east. He opens the black velvet curtains of the ark and reveals the Torah scroll. Esther takes a deep breath as he transfers it to her arms, as she turns toward the congregation and places the scroll carefully on the *bima*. Esther did it!

The rabbi rolls the scroll to the right place, and with the *yad*, the ceremonial Torah pointer that keeps them from touching the parchment, they chant their portion together. Do they make mistakes? Perhaps. But if Shira makes a mistake, Esther fixes it. And if Esther makes a mistake, Shira is there to support her. They fit together like salami and mustard.

Amen!

With a *mazel tov* and a congratulatory kiss on the *keppie* for them both, Rabbi Epstein sits.

The congregation is hushed.

Esther begins their speech, her voice strong. "This week's Torah portion urges children to obey their parents as they would obey God."

"But if any of you saw the *Nicky Sanders Show* this week, you know that Esther and I aren't so good at obeying our parents. In fact, we were so bad . . ." Shira sets it up.

"How bad were we?"

Shira grins at Esther's new confidence. "So bad, that we traded places! We switched lives! And our parents didn't even know we were gone."

There is a rumble of surprise and laughter through the congregation.

"And while we'll be making amends for our behavior for a long time," Esther continues after the congregation quiets, "we disobeyed our parents because we were obeying the dreams we held dear in our hearts."

"Sometimes, there are good reasons to break the rules," Shira continues. "Esther and I broke rules to save the Heights—"

"And," Esther adds quickly, "to raise our voices to God."

"Right, also that. But, we're not suggesting you should go around breaking rules willy-nilly. And we're not saying that God just sticks a desire in your soul and makes dreams come true easy peasy. Ohhhh, no. It takes a whole heaping casserole of hard work and patience, and you know what? It also takes a lot of luck. And—"

Esther elbows Shira in the ribs. "You're off script, Shir."

More laughter. Shira looks at Esther, her cousin, lucky to have found her at all. "Sorry, Ess. The point is, if you want a dream to come true, you might have to do something wrong. And if you're going to do something wrong—enjoy it."

Rose, whose lungs are stronger than ever, smiles from her wheelchair in the front of the sanctuary and gives them a thumbs-up.

"Ahem. The *point* is," Esther cuts in, shaking her head at Shira, her cousin, her new best friend. "A dream can be fragile. If we don't give it the care it needs—individually . . ."

"In families . . ." Shira continues.

"And in community," they both say together. "Then a dream has no chance at all." Esther reaches for Shira's hand behind the *bima* and squeezes.

Two years ago, two weeks ago, having a bat mitzvah was Esther's *only* dream. She had no idea there could be more—so much more than that. She looks out over the congregation at her theater family sitting side by side in the pews with her new synagogue family—Rabbi Epstein (who told her to call him Rabbi Sam), Rose, Frank, and Frank's wife. There are even Dutch tulips on the *bima* in Mona Epstein's memory. All this time, Esther thought a bat mitzvah would be her dream's destination, when really, it is the dawn of her next big dream. And who knows what that dream may be!

The sound of birdsong lilts through the windows to fill the silence after their speech, then the girls close their eyes, open their mouths, and sing "Oseh Shalom," a song for peace. They harmonize with each other, and their prayer envelopes the sanctuary and all of Idylldale.

At the service's end, when everyone congratulates the girls, Fanny approaches Rabbi Epstein. "The girls did beautifully."

"Young women, now."

"I didn't think it would mean much to me, but their words . . ." She stops, as if she can't find any of her own. "I didn't mean to deny . . ."

"Everyone worships in different ways," the rabbi says, his hand on her arm. "Your Esther taught me that. She is a true scholar. She has a beautiful brain."

"Thank you," she says, gripping his hand. "And I have to say—Shira is a talent. I've seen lots of young performers, and I know. This girl has a gift. *The* gift." She pauses. "But they're still in trouble, right? We agree on that?"

"Oh yes," he agrees.

"Excuse me," says a man with a bump on the bridge of his nose like Esther's.

Do you know who it is, *mayne kinder*?

Of course you do. It's Mel! Melvin Cooper, who hardly slept all night in his room at Scheinfeld's. He tossed and turned, nervous about reuniting with all he'd left behind. But he came to the bat mitzvah! Just like the girls promised, a dream that is nurtured sometimes does come true.

"Coop," Rabbi Epstein says. "I'm glad you made it!" He pumps Mel's hand and pulls him into an embrace. "You got our invitation?"

"An invitation?" Mel is bewildered. "No, that must have been lost in the post. I got a telegram. From Esther. My daughter, she tells me? Is it true?"

Fanny is all agog. "Mel . . . it is true. I'm so sorry." For now, she has the grace to step out of the way and point Mel toward the girls.

Esther sees him before Shira does and grabs Shira's arm to steady herself.

Salt and pepper, peanut butter and jelly, milk and cookies—long before Shira arrived, Esther and Fanny lived their lives as a pair. Now, Esther is overwhelmed to see what has been missing. Mel! Her father. She's not part of a pair, but a trio. More like a latke with sour cream and applesauce. And even though she doesn't know him, not yet, this new addition is filling a hole she'd thought would always be empty.

Mel walks toward her.

The first thing she notices is a star-shaped mole on *his* neck. She points to her own. "I have one too."

"What a miracle," Rabbi Epstein says.

Esther swallows and nods.

"Esther," Mel says, "when I got the telegram . . . when I saw the show on TV . . . Chicago is such a long drive . . . I left right away." He's flustered, and everything comes out in a tender rush. "Let me try again. I haven't been here, and I'm so sorry I missed out." Esther knows he's talking about missing more than the *Nicky Sanders Show*.

"Did you know about me?"

"I didn't, but I wish I had."

Mel offers Esther his hand to shake, but she embraces him with laughter and tears. Body and soul.

Fanny and Mel would have a lot to talk about later. But right now—a celebration!

At Scheinfeld's, Mel, Levi, Joshua, and Rabbi Epstein lift the girls on chairs as clarinet, violin, and accordion play raucous klezmer music. Their community dances circles around them, while Saul and I agree—yes, that's right!—that the brisket is as tasty as can be. Shira and Esther do an encore performance of their number from the *Nicky Sanders Show*, and Benny does a comedy bit that even makes Miss Scheinfeld laugh.

The clang of the trolley echoes throughout the hills and valleys of Idylldale. What will Shira and Esther dream up next? Does Shira end up on the stage? Will Esther someday lead her own congregation? What will happen to their newly joined family, to the Heights, or to Idylldale itself? Well, what do I know, *mayne kinder*? After all, I'm just the deli man.

THE END

CURTAIN CALL

MORTY'S GLOSSARY

If you've never taken a ride on the Idylldale trolley, then there's a better-than-average chance that you won't know some of the words in this book. That's okay. Many people don't understand much of what they hear or read, and they just nod their heads and smile when they could be learning. But those people are mostly grown-ups. Here's your chance to be smarter than they are.

ARK: The most sacred place in a synagogue that can be opened and closed, where the scrolls of the Torah are kept. Arks in the United States are generally on the eastern wall of the synagogue so that when congregants face the ark, they face Jerusalem. Some arks are a simple shelf with a curtain; others are a more elaborate and modern affair with remote-controlled moving electric doors, or stained glass.

BIMA: The pedestal or podium or raised platform in a synagogue where the service leader stands, and upon which the open Torah rests to be read by the rabbi or other members of the synagogue.

BISL: When my father used to ask my *bubbe* (see below) if she wanted a drink of wine with dinner, she'd say to my father, "Just a *bisl* wine. I don't want to be any trouble." And as a joke, my father would pour a teeny tiny bit of wine in her glass. And she would gasp and say, "*Oy*, that's too much."

BUBBE: Grandmother.

BUBBELE: Term of endearment or affection for a child or friend or the person you love.

BUPKES: Nada. Zilch. Nothing.

CHAI: The Hebrew letters that make up the word *chai* (or *life* in English) add up to eighteen. There is a Jewish tradition of gifting or donating money in increments of eighteen dollars. Scheinfeld's celebrates their thirty-sixth year, and when Esther gets the number thirty-six for her audition, she sees it as a good omen. Because what's better than *chai* but double *chai*!

CHALLAH: A braided loaf of bread that is used in the Sabbath ceremony on Friday night. If there are any leftovers Saturday morning, it makes wonderful French toast.

CHUTZPAH: If someone says that you have *chutzpah*, it could mean that you just did something very, very brave, very, very stupid, or some combination of the two. As in, "Did you see how she stood up to that bully?"

"I did. She's got *chutzpah*!"

FARBLUNGET: Technically, lost and wandering, but the word is also used when your state of mind or things around you are mixed up or confused.

HIGH HOLIDAYS: Rosh Hashanah and Yom Kippur mark the Jewish New Year (which is full of apples dipped in honey and joy) and the Day of Atonement (the day you ask for forgiveness and eat nothing at all). This is when the synagogue is most full. Is that because people store up all the bad things they've done for a whole a year before they say sorry? What do I know? I'm just a deli man.

KEPPIE: Your noodle, your noggin, your head. That loveliest part of you, perched on top of your neck, that holds all your thoughts, hopes, dreams, fears, and sadness. This word is a pinch of the Yiddish *kepele* and a dash of English. In my family, the mixing of Yiddish and English was called Yiddish/Yoddish. Other people call it Yinglish.

KISHKES: Literally, intestines. I'm not a nervous person generally, but there are some people (principals, bosses, my mother-in-law) or situations (a very difficult customer) that make my belly do double flips. That feeling is my *kishkes* in an uproar.

LEYN: The Yiddish word for the ceremonial chanting of Torah.

LOKSH / LOKSHN: Noodle/noodles. Our friend Benny has long arms and legs that look just like *lokshn*.

MAYNE KINDER: My children.

MAZEL TOV!: Congratulations! Applies to all the wonderful things in life: new babies, graduations, 100 percent on a test for which you studied hard, getting into your favorite college, winning a game or race, being cast after an audition, getting engaged or married, writing a book. What wonderful things have happened to you recently? Well, *mazel tov!*

MENSCH: A person of integrity or honor.

MESHUGE: Crazy. This isn't a mean thing. It's more about people who disagree with you. "The Yankees rule."

"What are you, *meshuge*? The Red Sox are the best baseball team ever."

It can also be affectionate. "You think I'm not your friend anymore? *Meshuge*."

NU: Sounds like "new" but often said with an upward lilt as if it had two syllables and not one. "n-U." It means "So?" or "Well?" But it can really be any question depending on the situation. If the same waiter is slow every time you go to the restaurant, you might say, "*Nu?*" and mean: "Of course that's how it is, nothing changes." Or, when you are waiting for a baby to be born and the doctor comes out of the delivery room but doesn't say anything right away and you say, "*Nu?*" what you mean is: "What's going on? Is everything okay?"

ONEG: While the full term is *oneg shabbat*, meaning "joy of the Sabbath," it's the social time after the Friday night service. Are there knishes, cakes, and cookies? Of course there are. What else is joy?

OY VEY/OY GEVALT: Oh no! Or, are you kidding me, or make it stop, or are you trying to kill your mother.

"*Oy*, this game of Monopoly just won't end!"

"*Oy*, this math problem is impossible!"

"*Oy*, enough with the *shmaltzy* songs."

"*Oy vey*, you still haven't cleaned your room? Bubbe arrives any minute!"

PISHER OR PISHEKER: Someone, like a baby who pees their pants, with very little experience or power.

PLOTZ: To burst with emotion.

REBBETZIN: The rabbi's wife.

SHLEP: Move or carry an object.

SHMALTZ: Technically, *shmaltz* is chicken fat, but it's also the Yiddish way of saying something is cheesy or overly sentimental.

SHPILKES: Literally, "pins," but here it means "on pins and needles" or "can't sit still." Ants in your pants.

SHTARKER: A strong person. In Levi's case, and traditionally, it's a tough guy who provides security, but when Benny comes by the deli, and I need someone to move boxes, I'll say, "Come here. I need a *shtarker* to *shlep* these boxes."

SHVITZING: Sweating.

SIDDUR: The prayer book used during a Jewish service. *Siddur* means "order." The book, like the Hebrew language, reads from right to left, so the back is the English front and the front is the English back.

SUKKAH: If you've ever made a fort in the woods, you've made something like a *sukkah*. Traditionally, they were temporary shelters the Jewish people made while wandering in the desert for forty years. During the holiday Sukkot, a congregation and/or some Jewish families will make a *sukkah* and take their meals in it. One side should be open, and the ceiling is often covered with branches in a way that allows you to still see the stars at night. You can decorate it with paper chains, dried corncobs, fall leaves, flowers, or anything else that celebrates the harvest.

TORAH: The first five books of the Old Testament that are further split into fifty-four smaller portions that are read each week in service.

TREYF: Food that is not kosher or goes against the dietary laws of Judaism outlined in the Torah. Remember my pork chop story in chapter twelve? Pork is *treyf*, so is shellfish, so is combining milk and meat (cheeseburgers aren't kosher).

TUCHUS: The thing you sit on. Your derriere, bum, backside, buttocks, bottom. The thing your parents wiped for years. And don't you forget it.

YAD: Hand, or a ceremonial Torah pointer that helps the reader keep their place. A *yad* has a decorative hand with an outstretched finger at the end of the pointer shaft.

AUTHOR'S NOTE

On a trip to the Society of Illustrators in the spring of 2014, I happened upon an exhibition of Drew Friedman's book *Old Jewish Comedians*. I hadn't gone there to see it, but one drawing and explanation card caught my eye. It was about a comedian, Benjamin Zuckerman, whose father wanted him to be a rabbi, but he wanted to be a comedian. *What if,* I thought, *there were two kids and they each wanted what the other had?* In this way, the seed of this book was planted.

The research for the book was long and winding. I read about funny Jewish women in the Jewish Women's Archive, I took a Yiddish theater class through YIVO Institute for Jewish

Research, I interviewed family members, and I watched lots and lots of videos of comedians and performers from a bygone era.

Some of my first readers were curious about the when and the where of the book. I had a very specific image in mind for the two different worlds that made up Idylldale. Esther's world would be set in a space like the Lower East Side of New York City. This space would be dense with Jewish working-class people, tenement apartment dwellers, and Yiddish performers. Shira's space would be more like the resorts that used to be popular in the Catskill Mountains called the Borscht Belt. For more on the Borscht Belt resorts, see *Growing Up at Grossinger's*, by Tania Grossinger, or listen to Jen Stewart's podcast *The Borscht Belt Tattler*.

The when of this story was a little more difficult. In Idylldale, the transportation, fashion, electronics, and television are vaguely set in the late 1940s, but I've borrowed from other earlier time periods for the neighborhood around the Heights.

In 1910 and after World War I, numerous Yiddish theaters opened, including the Second Avenue Theater in 1911, the National Theater in 1912, the Yiddish Art Theatre in 1926, and the Public Theater in 1927. Before a sharp audience decline in 1930, there were twelve Yiddish theaters in New York and twelve more around the country, with 120,000 people attending over a thirty-eight-week season. The influx of immigrants from Eastern Europe included Jewish people who brought the Yiddish language with them. In America, Yiddish theater exposed them to classic and American stories told in a distinctly Jewish way while keeping them connected to their culture.

But in the Great Depression, the president, Herbert Hoover, severely limited the numbers of people allowed to enter the United States, arguing that there weren't enough jobs for new immigrants. This change meant that there were fewer Yiddish speakers coming to the United States.

With the rise of the German Nazis in the 1930s, and the rise of antisemitism in the United States during the same period, Jewish people were more likely to assimilate, or blend in, than to celebrate our culture. What followed was World War II, the Holocaust, and the genocide of six million Jewish people in Europe. Antisemitism in the United States at that time was also the catalyst for the success of hotels and cottages like Scheinfeld's Resort and Cottages. Jewish people were banned from many resorts and hotels, so they opened their own.

Many books for children and young adults that feature Jewish protagonists are about the Holocaust, history, or holidays. I wanted to write a story full of Jewish joy and laughter without the drumbeat that linked my identity to constant oppression. And while I never wanted this to be a book about the Holocaust, I did want to highlight the declining audiences for Yiddish theater through the 1930s that led to all but four theaters being closed by 1945, and the rise of television shows hosted by Ed Sullivan and Jack Benny (the models for Nicky Sanders), which turned Borscht Belt stand-up comics like Jerry Lewis (the physical comedy model for Benny Bell) into stars. For more, see Lawrence J. Epstein's *The Haunted Smile: The Story of Jewish Comedians in America.*

The funny women often get missed. In this book, the name Red Hot Fanny is an homage to Sophie Tucker (nicknamed the "Last of the Red Hot Mamas") and Fanny Brice. I first heard Fanny Brice as her character Baby Snooks when I was nine years old, on a cassette tape my father had. I laughed so hard that I played the tape over and over. Biographies of these women can be found on the Jewish Women's Archive website.

A note about vaudeville: The connections between Yiddish theater and vaudeville are strong, and that means that one has to consider the racism of their predecessor, the minstrel show. Racial and ethnic impersonations through the use of blackface were not unusual, but they were and are racist. If you are interested in learning more about that aspect of vaudeville, I suggest the Jewish Women's Archive article "Vaudeville in the United States," by Peter Antelyes: https://jwa.org/encyclopedia/article/vaudeville-in-united-states.

ACKNOWLEDGMENTS

This is the part of the book where I get to say thank you. And holy casserole, there are so many people who helped make my dream debut. How many people? So many that if you gave them a standing ovation while I read their names, your legs would get tired and your hands might fall off.

First, a massive thank you to my agent, Janine Le, who believed in this manuscript and believes in the dreams to come.

I will be forever grateful to my double dream team editors: Taylor Norman fell in love with this book and my brain (the best compliment ever) and is not only an editor but also an amazing educator; Daria Harper helped hone the story, highlight the Jewish joy, and shepherd the book to launch.

Thanks to the entire Chronicle Books team: Ginee Seo, Claire Fletcher, Kevin Armstrong, Andie Krawcyzk, Mary Duke, Caitlin Ek, Mikaela Luke, Carrie Gao, and Lucy Medrich (thank you for dotting my i's and crossing my t's). Thank you to Marco Guadalupi for a joyful cover that jumps off the shelves, and to Jay Marvel and Kathryn Li for designing the book of my dreams.

My parents, my grandmother, and her sisters wove Yiddish/Yoddish phrases into the English of my early childhood, but I didn't know until I was much older that 1) they were another language and 2) not everyone else knew them. I never read or wrote Yiddish, so I'm grateful to the Facebook "Learn Yiddish" group members, especially Sefra Burstin for her help translating Shira and Esther's song, and to the "Jewish Kidlit Mavens" group, specifically Sharon Abra Hanen for discussing the similarities and differences between Yiddish and Hebrew. Any mistakes in grammar or transliteration ultimately are my own.

My family at Vermont College of Fine Arts: Faculty, students, staff, and administration nurtured and grew my dream. When I'd only written the prologue, Martine Leavitt's encouragement at that long-ago retreat kept me writing this story. Alan Cumyn helped me find my voice and taught me to say no to the things that sidetrack me from my writing. My entire League of Extraordinary Cheese Sandwich class gave me a lasting community. Melanie Crowder, Meg Wiviott, and Kathy Wilson, your love and friendship kept me focused and committed to the dream at our roving writing retreats. Thanks to Susan Korchak, Lyn Miller-Lachman, Katie Bartlett, Shelley Saposnik, Patti Brown, and Mary-Walker Wright for the manuscript swaps and critiques. Thanks to Erin Baldwin, who stopped making pancakes on a Saturday morning to chat with me about omniscient narrators.

Thanks to my online New York quarantine writing friends Shira Schindel, Rebecca Kelliher, and Cleo Levin, and to

Angele McQuade, who reminds me to have a self-care goal too.

'Ihank you to SCBWI, especially my Maine and New England friends, for the keynotes, workshops, conferences, and most of all the community. To the Schmoozers: Cynthia Lord, Jo Knowles, Tamra Wight, Joyce Shor Johnson, Mona Pease, Cindy Faughnan, Laura Ludwig Hamor, Valerie Giogas, Denise Ortakales, Mary Morton Cowan, Jeanne Bracken, Nancy Cooper, and Megan Frazer Blakemore, may our paths cross again soon and let there be cake.

I'm grateful to have worked at two wonderful independent bookstores. Thank you to my coworkers and the owners of Books of Wonder and Politics & Prose and to all the wonderful booksellers who connect children with "just right" books every day.

Thanks to Jennifer Powers, Ellen Schein, Kathy Thorson, Debbi Atwood, Kim Simmons, Rachel Lowe, Penny Wheeler-Abbot, Ellen McPherson, Katherine Pellatreau,

Mona Panici, Tracey Falla, Kellie Otis, and Leslie Zampetti for the late-night phone calls, long walks, tears, and hugs.

To my sister, Rebecca, and my brothers, Nick and Sam, love always.

This book is dedicated to my mother and father, Ruth and Dan Jordan. My father died before he could see the fruits of my labors, but he was the first to teach me to craft beautiful things with my hands and my imagination. May his memory be a blessing. I will never be able to thank my mother for all she has done, but she was the first to teach me that the first draft is never the last draft. Thank you for the love, the dinners, the pride, the joy.

The book is also dedicated to my creative, kind, generous, brilliant, beautiful sons, Isaac and Ethan. You are the most supportive fans and best story brainstormers I could ever ask for. Every day, I'm honored to be your mother.